Praise for Linda Goodnight

"Goodnight's emotion-packed story celebrates accepting life with its laughter, sorrow and love."
—*RT Book Reviews* on *The Baby Bond*

"A truly inspiring story of overcoming trying circumstances and discovering personal strength."
—*RT Book Reviews* on *The Last Bridge Home*

"This is a touching story that will renew the reader's holiday spirit and belief in miracles."
—*RT Book Reviews* on *The Christmas Child*

Praise for Lissa Manley

"Wonderful chemistry between the main characters makes this a delightful story with a couple of sweet secondary romances."
—*RT Book Reviews* on *Family to the Rescue*

"[A] smart, touching story about two people who have every reason to resist love… Strong, sympathetic characters, realistic situations and a charming setting set this novel apart."
—*RT Book Reviews* on *In a Cowboy's Arms*

"[P]lenty of twists and turns along with enough laughter to keep readers interested in Lissa Manley's inventive plot."
—*RT Book Reviews* on *The Bachelor Chronicles*

LINDA GOODNIGHT

Winner of a RITA® Award for excellence in inspirational fiction, Linda Goodnight has also won a Booksellers' Best Award, an ACFW Book of the Year award and a Reviewers' Choice Award from *RT Book Reviews*. Linda has appeared on the Christian bestseller list and her romance novels have been translated into more than a dozen languages. Active in orphan ministry, this former nurse and teacher enjoys writing fiction that carries a message of hope and light in a sometimes dark world. She and her husband, Gene, live in Oklahoma. Readers can write to her at linda@lindagoodnight.com, or c/o Love Inspired Books, 233 Broadway, Suite 1001, New York, NY 10279.

LISSA MANLEY

decided she wanted to be a published author at the ripe old age of twelve. She read her first romance novel as a teenager when a neighbor gave her a box of old books, and she quickly decided romance was her favorite genre. Although she still enjoys digging into a good medical thriller.

When her youngest was still in diapers, Lissa needed a break from strollers and runny noses, so she sat down and started crafting a romance, and she has been writing ever since. Nine years later, she sold her first book, fulfilling her childhood dream. She feels blessed to be able to write what she loves, and intends to be writing until her fingers quit working or she runs out of heartwarming stories to tell. She's betting the fingers will go first.

Lissa lives in the beautiful city of Portland, Oregon, with her wonderful husband of twenty-seven years, a grown daughter and college-aged son, and two bossy poodles who rule the house and get away with it. When she's not writing, she enjoys reading, crafting, bargain hunting, cooking and decorating. She loves hearing from her readers and can be reached through her website, www.lissamanley.com, or through Love Inspired Books.

A Snowglobe Christmas

Linda Goodnight
and
Lissa Manley

Love Inspired

 ™ LOVE INSPIRED BOOKS

Recycling programs for this product may not exist in your area.

ISBN-13: 978-0-373-87777-5

A SNOWGLOBE CHRISTMAS

Copyright © 2012 by Harlequin Books S.A.

The publisher acknowledges the copyright holders of the individual works as follows:

YULETIDE HOMECOMING
Copyright © 2012 by Linda Goodnight

A FAMILY'S CHRISTMAS WISH
Copyright © 2012 by Melissa A. Manley

CONTENTS

YULETIDE HOMECOMING

Linda Goodnight

In memory of my brother, Stan Case.
I miss you, bro.

Cause me to hear your loving kindness
in the morning, for in you do I trust.
—*Psalms* 143:8

Chapter One

High above Snowglobe, Montana, Amy Caldwell's blue Ford Focus wound round and round the narrow road as she made her way into the valley nestled snugly between two snow-capped mountains. As if the creative hand of God had reached down and given the earth a loving shake, snow swirled upward in a constant circle so the small picturesque village of tiny stores and houses was forever captured in time and space like a snowglobe.

The colorful scatter of buildings and snow-kissed evergreens rested inside a bowl of milk-white snow. Smoke curled from rooftops and pulled Amy in like a long-lost friend. Her heart leaped at the sight.

"Home." The word tasted foreign on her tongue. If all went as planned, she was home to stay.

Time and distance and a growing faith may not have healed the heartache she'd left behind, but it was time to let go, to come home, to do this one thing that her mother asked. At least she would no longer have to face Rafe Westfield and his betrayal.

When her car reached the village, she turned onto Main Street and headed straight for The Snowglobe Gift Shoppe. She parked in a slant at the curb and slammed out of the car, eager as her boots crunched on fresh, powdery snow. Before she reached the glass-fronted shop, a slender woman in dark slacks and a red scoop neck pullover rushed out the door, her shoulder-length black hair flying.

"Mom!" Amy said just as she was enveloped in a hug that smelled of hothouse roses and potpourri. At fifty, Dana Caldwell's Spanish rose beauty still made Amy wish she looked more like her mom and less like her absentee father, the golden boy who had turned out to have brass feet.

"You made it. I was starting to worry."

Amy smiled. Her mother always said that. "Safe and sound. And excited."

"Are you? Oh, honey, I'm so ready to retire."

"Semi-retire. You're not leaving me alone with this store."

Dana laughed. "Well, not yet. But you know the retail gift business as well as I do. Better. You have a degree!"

The degree in marketing meant more to her mom than it did to Amy or to her employers in Spokane. Former employers, she thought with a happy little step as her mom looped their arms together and tugged her into the shop.

Gently played symphonic Christmas music practically sucked her inside, alluring and lovely. Amy closed her eyes and breathed deeply of the warm, welcoming scent of Christmas past and present. "I love this smell."

For as long as she could remember, cinnamon and pine, snow and flowers, and this shop with snowglobes and poinsettias in the vast picture window had meant Christmas.

"Christmas is the best smell of the year."

They both giggled and hugged once more, a spontaneous action Amy knew would be repeated time and again. Her mama was a hands-on kind of woman.

Amy stepped away from her mother's embrace to survey the gloriously decorated store.

"The shop looks amazing." She turned a slow circle, examining every detail. "I don't think I've ever seen it look bet—"

The word died an abrupt death, jammed down into her throat like a fist.

"Hello, Amy." The gently masculine voice was as familiar as Christmas and as unwelcome as a lump of coal.

Amy's heart jerked against her rib cage.

Rafe Westfield, the man who'd taken her heart and then handed it back again, leaned against the glass-topped counter. Bundled to the ears in a sheepskin jacket, and out of place amidst the singing Santas and dainty angels, he was handsomer than ever. His brown hair had grown out from the last time she'd seen him, after the recruiter had buzzed him bald, and now lay in gentle waves above a forehead no longer smooth and boyish but creased with fine worry lines. If anything they made him more rugged, more delicious.

Like his mouth. He had the most perfect lips a man could have, the bottom full and curved with the top a long, low M like the mountains surrounding Snowglobe. She remembered the feel of that mouth, the kisses they'd shared when he'd loved her. Or claimed to. He never really had; she knew that now. If he'd loved her, he would not have joined the military against her wishes.

She licked her own lips, gone bone-dry.

"Rafe?" she managed. "What are *you* doing here?"

She'd worked hard to let go of the bitterness, to forgive and move on, but in one moment, the old feelings came rushing back like a tidal wave.

"I live here," he said. Below a slash of dark brows, his winter-blue eyes were solemn and aloof. The sparkle was gone, the teasing glint, the ready smile. He had changed. But then, so had she. Amy was no longer the gullible little college grad who'd dreamed of nothing but being Mrs. Rafe Westfield and making a home in Snowglobe, Montana.

"No, you don't," she insisted. "You can't live here. You're in the marines. You're in the Middle East somewhere."

"Was. Now I'm home."

Home? He was calling Snowglobe home? The flutter of panic that had started way down in Amy's belly soared through her bloodstream. He couldn't be here permanently. Not if she was.

"What happened to your military career?"

The career that was more important than a life with me.

A muscle above one cheekbone flinched. It was the only indication that her question had hit a sore spot.

"Three tours was enough." Abruptly he turned to the counter and collected two giant pots of scarlet poinsettias. To her mother, he said, "I'll drop these off on my way."

"Thanks for doing that, Rafe. The shop's so busy, I'm not sure when I could get out there."

"No problem."

Then, exactly as he had five years ago, he turned and walked out the door.

"Mother!" Amy spun around, fingers gripping the counter's edge. "What is he doing here?"

With mild reproof Dana said, "You're repeating yourself, Amy. Rafe has lived in Snowglobe all his life, just as you have."

"That's not true. He left. He said he wasn't coming back. Why didn't you tell me?"

Her mother pretended to rearrange a lighted ceramic village behind the cash register. "If I recall—and I do—you forbade me to ever speak his name again. You said the relationship was done and over with and you wanted to move on. And you did."

"You should have told me anyway," Amy answered, feeling unreasonable and petulant.

"Would you have come home? Would you have agreed to take over the shop?"

"No, I wouldn't have. I don't want to be constantly reminded of how he humiliated me. It's hard enough to come back to Snowglobe knowing that everyone in town pitied poor little Amy Caldwell when Rafe broke off our engagement to join the military."

"Oh, precious girl." Her mom repositioned a jingling reindeer before taking Amy by the shoulders. "That was a long time ago. You've enjoyed a nice career, friends, dates, travel. If you'd married so young, look at what you would have missed. I thought you'd forgiven and forgotten all about Rafe Westfield."

"I said I've forgiven him. I'll never forget. How could I? We were engaged. I'd picked out a dress!"

She'd loved him so much she thought she'd die when he chose the marines over her. Yet, he had, and there was no changing the past. After six months of feeling sorry for herself and dealing with the pitying stares, she'd taken the job in Spokane. She'd found a good church, made friends, had a great life.

So why was she letting Rafe get to her now?

The internal question shook her. Why indeed? Rafe Westfield was nothing but a bad memory.

The tiny bell over the shop door jingled and two customers entered. Her mother moved into action, leaving Amy to wander through the beautiful Christmas displays. Maybe the sights and smells would calm her stress and bring back the excitement of being home.

She shucked her jacket, leaving the bright turquoise scarf to dangle over her long black sweater.

She didn't understand why she was so upset. She was completely over Rafe. He was old news. It wasn't like she hadn't had a boyfriend in the past five years. She had and yet, the old hurt had flown in her face like an out of control downhiller.

She rounded the corner of the greeting card display and heard someone say, "Amy? Is that you? I heard you were coming home for Christmas."

"Katie?" Amy's mood rose at the sight of her bouncy blonde friend from high school. With a squeal, the two women exchanged a brief hug. "It's so good to see you. What are you doing?"

"Trying to find the perfect birthday card for Todd." Katie had married a local boy right out of high school. "I'm having a little Christmas-style birthday party in his honor on Saturday. Why don't you come? It'll be a great way to see old friends again."

"I'd love to! Are you sure it's okay? I don't want to be a fifth wheel."

Katie made a noise in the back of her throat. "Stop. This is Snowglobe. No one is a fifth wheel here. Bring a little gift for the gift exchange if you want. It'll be fun."

"Are you playing Dirty Santa?"

Katie fingered a particularly pretty birthday card before putting it back on the shelf and selecting one with a grinning mule on the front. "We play Nice Santa, sort of. All the gifts are decent, but some are great. No one loses, but it's lots of fun to see the guys in a friendly fight over a new snowboard and the girls bartering for a gift certificate to Molly's Massage."

"Mmm. Molly's Massage." Amy rotated her shoulders, tight after the unexpected confrontation with Rafe. "Sounds wonderful. I'm in."

"Last year I ended up with a set of deer antler salt and pepper shakers." Katie laughed. "Todd thought they were so cool!"

Amy laughed, too, feeling much better after reconnecting with her old friend. When Katie left, a steady stream of customers entered the shop, most of them people Amy knew, though a few tourists had already begun to gather for the annual Christmas ski race. Vacationers usually rented cabins and lodges in the countryside or stayed at the Snowglobe Bed-and-Breakfast, eager to catch the spirit of a small-town Christmas in the snowy Rockies.

Amy fell into the familiar rhythm of working the store, aware that business was brisk. But no matter how busy they were, she kept picturing her handsome, rugged ex-fiancé leaning against the glass counter.

During a lull, her mother said, "There's mulled cider in the urn. Let's grab a cup while we can."

"Got any cookies to go with it?"

"Gingerbread from Porter's Bakery. Becka made it fresh this morning."

"Oh, yum." They headed to the back corner of the store where a silver urn brewed something year-round according to the season. For Christmas, the small table was draped with green linen brightened by red napkins and Spode Christmas tree China. The centered urn emitted the warm, cozy smell of spiced cider, and beneath a glass cake stand sugar-sprinkled slices of gingerbread tempted the shopper to linger. In the background, a recorded harpist strummed "White Christmas."

Dana Caldwell was a master at presentation.

"Aren't you glad you're home?" her mother asked, handing her a steaming mug complete with cinnamon stick.

"I am, Mom. Really," she said when Dana pressed her lips together in the mother's sign of concern.

"Goodness. After your reaction to Rafe, I was afraid you might back out on me. I can't wait to turn this shop over to you and kick up my heels a little."

"Mom? Kick up your heels?"

A rosy flush darkened her mother's cheeks. "I don't mean

go wild, but I would like to travel and do some things while I'm still healthy and young enough."

Amy lifted the steaming mug to her lips and sipped, thinking. As a child, she'd never considered her mother as anyone but a mom and shopkeeper. Now, as an adult, she was a little taken aback to realize her mom might want something more, something for herself.

"I guess running the shop tied you down."

"Don't think I'm complaining. I love this shop. God provided a way for me to raise my daughter and make a living without shortchanging either, and working with beautiful things is right up my alley. But now, *you* need this place. And I don't. I'm so glad you're here to take over, and I pray this shop is as wonderful to you as it has been to me."

"You're incredible, you know that?" Wasn't it sad that she'd waited twenty-eight years to realize such a thing?

With a smile, her mother fluttered a hand. "You weren't thinking that a few minutes ago when Rafe was here."

"Not true. I've always known I have an exceptional mother." She stirred the cinnamon stick around in the mug. "Rafe was the past. I can't let his presence ruin this homecoming."

Dana took two thick slices of gingerbread and slid them onto China saucers. "That's my girl. No looking back."

Exactly. She hoped.

As they settled into the dainty chairs with their snacks, Amy turned her thoughts from herself to her mother. After Amy's father had left, Dana Caldwell had thrown herself into the store without complaint, making it better than ever. She must have been devastated by Dad's betrayal, but Amy had been too young and heartbroken to consider anyone else's feelings. Now she saw things in a different light. Like King David in the Bible, her mom had grieved the loss. Then she'd wiped her tears, set her eyes on the future and moved on, never looking back at what she could not change.

Was that what God expected her to do? Even with Rafe living in the same town?

She took a nibble of the spiced bread, thinking about how she had changed in the past five years. She'd grown up, grown closer to the Lord. She'd been so ready to come home and take over the shop. She couldn't let her mother down.

But she hadn't reckoned on Rafe.

Chapter Two

By closing time, Amy was in the swing of things at the gift shop. She'd made sales, wrapped gifts with shiny foiled papers and voluminous colored ribbons, unpacked the new stock of handcrafted glass ornaments and delivered flowers to New Life Church.

At the latter, she'd enjoyed a chat with Pastor Jacobson and allowed herself, with little effort, to be persuaded to help with the charity food basket preparation and delivery.

"I've always loved doing the Blessing Baskets," she'd told her mother when she'd returned to the shop.

Dana was cleaning up, setting the shop to rights for closing time. With a smile, she said, "It's a good thing to do and the interaction will put you right back in the heart of Snowglobe's Christmas celebrations."

"That's what I was thinking." Amy took the bottle of Windex from her mother's hands and spritzed the glass countertop. "Pastor says he's had more applications for help than ever this year."

"Times are difficult for many people. That's why it's important to do what we can. Some towns have angel trees. In Snowglobe we have food and gift baskets."

"Apparently the church has had a mountain of donations

but not enough volunteers signed up to help sort, box and deliver. Pastor seemed thrilled that I wanted to."

"Interesting. I know several who've mentioned helping. In fact…" Mom's voice trailed away and she got a strange expression on her face.

"What?"

Her mother reclaimed the Windex bottle and grabbed a paper towel. Without answering, she crossed to the plate glass window and spritzed, rubbing the pane with all her might.

"Mom." Amy carefully pushed aside a box of glass ornaments and followed her mother. "What's the deal? Why are you acting weird?"

Outside the gleaming windows, the sidewalk shone dark and damp beneath golden street lamps adorned with red bows. Snowflakes swirled fat and lazy like falling feathers. Cars motored down the streets past other businesses dressed for the holidays. The tiny town of Snowglobe was a Christmas fantasy, a wish come true.

Inside the warm, sweet-smelling gift shop, Dana lowered the Windex bottle and turned slowly to meet her daughter's gaze. "Did Pastor Jacobson mention who was in charge of the Blessing Basket drive this year?"

"I thought Pastor was."

"No, he's not. Rafe is."

"Rafe!"

Two people passed the shop windows and slowed to admire the display of a snowy lighted village.

"Working with Rafe won't be a problem, will it?"

Amy swallowed past the protest rising like a volcano. Work with Rafe? In the same room? For hours on end?

"No," she managed. "No problem at all."

Returning from a test drive, Rafe parked the snowmobile in the maintenance bay of Westfield Sports Rentals and dismounted. He pulled off his goggles and helmet, hanging them on the back wall with the rows of similar rental equipment.

His younger brother, Jake, exited the office and strode in his direction. Brotherly love swelled in Rafe's chest. If not for Jake, he would have arrived home another jobless vet. But before he'd left for the marines, while he was still licking his wounds over losing Amy, he and Jake had come up with the idea of opening a sports rental business. With Rafe's money, thanks to several years of combat pay, Jake had done the hard work of building the business from the ground up. Knowing this business and his little brother were depending on him had given Rafe something to focus on when war had threatened to overwhelm.

He'd told Jake none of this, of course. But he was grateful.

"How'd she do?" Jake asked, nodding toward the Polaris. In jeans and pullover sweater, he looked like the college man he would be if not for the shop. Good-looking guy, even if Rafe did say so himself. Dark curly hair, blue eyes and a grin that warned the onlooker he was up to something. Mom claimed her sons looked alike but Rafe figured Jake won the handsome dog contest.

"The carburetor's still not right," Rafe answered.

"I'll break it down tomorrow. There must be some sludge buildup in one of the jets."

"That's what I was thinking." Rafe fell into step with his brother and returned to the office, a cozy room that served as both business center and customer service area. Rock music boomed from the piped-in stereo. "You gotta change that to Christmas music."

Jake shrank back in horror. "A steady dose of smarmy muzak about chestnuts and reindeer? Dude! That stuff poisons the soul."

Rafe grinned a little at his brother's over-the-top reaction. "Customers like it."

Jake gripped his throat and made a strangling sound.

"Deal with it. Customer service and all that." Rafe tapped a fist against his brother's shoulder. "Besides, a dose of real Christmas would be *good* for your soul, not poison."

"Brother, you're scaring me. You've turned into an old man."

The comment, meant as a sibling jest, struck a tender spot. Jake didn't get it. He hadn't been where Rafe had been. He hadn't seen and done and heard things that make a man ponder the important things in life. Rafe thanked God for that. And there was the crux. God. Like Rafe had been before joining the military, Jake's faith didn't mean much. He was morally a decent man. That was enough.

Or so Rafe had thought.

If there was one fact big brother had learned on the front lines, it was that men die with God on their lips. Some curse Him. Some call on Him.

The latter died in peace. Rafe still heard the former in his dreams.

The song changed to hard-driving heavy metal. He'd heard plenty of that in the desert, too.

Everyone needed a little Christmas with its promise of hope and peace. Especially him. If that made him an old man…

He turned down the stereo. "All the rentals back in for the day?"

"Two still out." Jake arched a black eyebrow toward the darkening sky. "Shouldn't be much longer. Wanna help me count the money?"

Rafe grinned. "Won't turn that down. You're making me a rich man."

Both brothers laughed. They were far from rich and, like most new businesses, struggled at times, but they were growing, too. Rafe moved behind the long, low counter that served as a desk. The counter reminded him of Dana Caldwell's gift shop. And Amy.

"You'll never guess who I ran into today," he said as casually as he could.

"Amy?"

He looked up in surprise. "News travels fast."

"That's a fact. So, how is she?"

Rafe let a beat pass while he thought about how to answer. Amy, in her jaunty knit beret with her warm smile and her voice breathy and excited, had stolen his senses the moment she'd sailed into The Snowglobe Gift Shoppe arm-in-arm with her mother. He'd had a minute to compose himself, to pretend he hadn't thought about her every day for the past five years, but her effect lingered with him still.

She looked the same with shaggy blond hair that flew around her face in wisps and honey-brown eyes she considered too small and plain for beauty. She was wrong about that. Amy sparkled.

He'd known she was coming home, had even prepared himself to see her again. At least he'd thought so.

"She's home to take over The Snowglobe Gift Shoppe," he said, pleased at how light and normal his voice sounded. "Dana told me."

"How do you feel about that?"

"How do I *feel?*" Rafe made a rude noise. "You sound like a psychiatrist. How I feel about anything doesn't mean squat."

"Yeah, yeah. Tell it to someone who doesn't know better." Jake clapped him on the shoulder. "I was there, dude. Remember?"

Rafe kept his head down, sorting rental receipts into neat stacks. "Ancient history."

"She broke your heart."

"I broke hers." Amy had wanted to get married before he left for the military. He'd wanted to wait. He was still fuzzy on the particulars but at some point, they'd fought until she'd handed him his ring.

"Reciprocal stupidity if you ask me."

"I didn't. We made the right decision." If he'd been killed in combat, Amy would have been a widow. He couldn't bear the thought of what that would have done to her. Or worse, what if she'd had a baby? A fatherless baby to raise by herself. The break-up was the best gift he could give her before he left.

"That was then," Jake said. "This is now."

"My brother the philosopher."

"So, when are you going to ask her out?"

Rafe's heart jerked. Ask her out? "She wasn't exactly excited to see me."

"Ask her anyway."

"I'll pass." No use digging up dry bones.

Jake slid the cash receipts into a zippered bag for the night deposit at the bank. "You still in love with her?"

"You're not going to let this go, are you?" Rafe made a notation on the paper pad. Later, he'd do the data entry on the computer.

"Can't. My big brother spent four years of his life making the world a better place. I want him to be happy."

Rafe grunted. Little brother knew how to get to him. "I *am* happy. This business makes me happy. Being home makes me happy." He cast an eye toward the stereo. "Christmas music would make me happier."

Jake snorted but didn't go away. "Amy's pretty hot-looking. Nice girl. So…just to be clear on the subject. If I ask her out, you'd be okay with it?"

Before Rafe could stop the reaction, he was up and out of his chair, scowling at his little brother over the counter.

A slow, knowing smile spread over Jake's face. "Gotcha."

Chapter Three

Amy's boots echoed in the empty hall between the side door and the family center at the back of New Life Church. All day long she'd felt jittery about coming tonight. Now, to make her even jumpier, the church seemed unusually quiet. She'd expected a crowd to help sort the boxes of donated foods and gifts, and to act as a buffer between her and her ex-fiancé.

Slipping her gloves from her fingers, she stuffed them into her pockets and rolled her suddenly stiff shoulders. As she entered the large common room, Pastor Jacobson spotted her and came forward, his ruddy face open and smiling.

"Amy, you made it." He offered his hand, swallowing hers in his much larger one. The forty-something former pro wrestler was the size of Paul Bunyan with an equally big heart.

She returned the smile and unwound a thick scarf from her neck. "I must be early. Where is everyone?"

"You may be it," he said. "A scout troop was scheduled for tonight but something's going on at the school and they canceled. With time short, we're falling behind, so Rafe comes in most nights for a few hours. You're a blessing for volunteering to help him."

Blessing? She sure didn't feel that way, and when Rafe

appeared from the kitchen area toting a box labeled "green beans," she wished she'd not come at all.

"No one else volunteered?"

"A few others may pop in. You never know." Pastor patted her shoulder. "Now, if you'll excuse me, I'm headed over to the hospital. Sadie took a fall. Keep her in your prayers."

Amy stared in dismay at the pastor's departing back. Just like that, she was alone with Rafe Westfield. All day she'd considered backing out. Now she wished she had. But when she'd mentioned working late at the gift shop, her mom had pushed her out the door.

Behind her, Rafe slammed a box onto a table. Amy spun around.

"Hi," he said, calm as could be. "Thanks for volunteering. We're shorthanded."

Amy swallowed a flutter of nerves. "So I see."

"Might as well take off your coat and get comfortable. There's a lot to do."

Get comfortable? That was not likely to happen. But she shed her coat and hat, wondering how she'd gotten into this miserable situation.

"Look, I—uh…" She pressed her lips together, trying to think of a reason to leave but nothing came. The truth was she loved this project, had volunteered all through high school and beyond. Why should she allow an unimportant man to take that pleasure from her the way he'd taken her heart? With a soft exhale, she said, "Tell me where to start."

She could do this. She *would* do this. Rafe didn't need to know how awkward she felt. Or that the anger and resentment of their broken engagement simmered just beneath the surface of civility. Resentment she'd thought was long gone.

Rafe zipped a knife along the top of a box and flipped up the flaps.

"We set up empties on those tables," he said, pointing,

"and the finished ones over there. And these are the donated items to pull from."

"Just like always."

"Yes. Like old times."

Old times? She didn't think so. In old times, this would have been fun. They would have laughed and teased and made a game of sorting and packing. He would have tossed a bag of rice at her and later, when he wasn't looking, she would have taped his shoe to the floor. Between the pranks and hijinks, they would have talked about any and everything and planned their holiday adventures.

Those times were as gone as their love.

Stiff as a mid-January icicle, Amy took a list and began sorting through random items donated by service groups and individuals. Several minutes passed while neither spoke. The tension in Amy's neck tightened. She was intensely aware of Rafe's every movement, of being alone with him for the first time since their break-up. The huge, mostly empty hall echoed with painful silence, except for the rattle of cans and scrape of boxes. She could even hear herself swallow!

"A-w-k-w-a-r-d," she muttered to a can of yams.

"Did you say something?"

Amy didn't look up. She didn't need to look to know Rafe was burning her with a questioning stare. "Nothing."

Tin cans clattered against the brown Formica tabletops while she repeated her mantra. She was doing this for Jesus and the needy. Rafe could go take a leap in a snowbank. She didn't like him. He'd left her, broken her heart. She could work beside him for the sake of others. He would not affect her.

As if he read her thoughts, Rafe moved his half-filled box directly across from hers so they were standing face-to-face. His gray-blue eyes searched hers. "You all right?"

"Fine."

He nodded, all the while stacking canned goods into a box.

with automated efficiency. Tension simmered. If he didn't feel it and get the message that she didn't want to talk to him, he was an insensitive slob.

"Snowglobe's a great place to be during the holidays," he said, rattling boxes of macaroni and cheese.

Really? Then why had he left? "It's a great place to be any time."

If he comprehended the jab, he dodged it. "Spokane must have agreed with you."

"What?" Frowning, she glanced up. "Why?"

"You look good."

"Oh. Well. Thanks. I enjoyed the time there."

"Your mother seems really happy to have you home."

"She is." *Now shut up and leave me alone. And stop looking at me as if you're even the slightest bit interested in my life.*

"Are you happy about taking over the shop?"

Amy suppressed a sigh. He was as insensitive as she'd thought. "For the most part. I've missed the small-town things we do at Christmas. The tree lighting, caroling door-to-door."

"I'm looking forward to those myself. The ski race, too."

She resisted the urge to ask why he'd changed his mind and come home. She didn't want to care why he did anything.

When she didn't speak, another uncomfortable silence fell. With an inner groan, Amy wondered which was worse, talking to Rafe or dealing with the awkward silence.

She stacked four cans of corn into a box and stole a glance toward the doorway. Not another soul anywhere around.

When she could bear the quiet no longer, she asked, "Are you competing?"

"In the race?" He shook his head. "No, but Jake is. I'm minding the store. The recreational rental business should be brisk when tourists hit town."

"So, how's that working out for you?"

With a box of stuffing in each hand, he grinned, transforming his serious expression into a thing of beauty. Thick lines radiated from the corner of his eyes, lines that hadn't been there five years ago. A pinch of concern prodded Amy. She wasn't stupid or uninformed. She knew where he'd been for most of his military career, and now she wondered what kind of toll war had taken on the breezy young athlete she remembered.

"I play with big boys' toys all day," he said. "Can't beat a job like that."

She studied him, bothered by her thoughts and this sudden, unwanted curiosity about his life. "Business must be good."

"We're doing all right. You should come by sometime and check us out. Take a spin on one of the new Arctic Cats." Using a black marker, he labeled a filled box and set it aside.

"Maybe I'll do that." When Antarctica melts. Though she was itching to ask why he'd left the military, she refrained, struggling not to care one way or the other. But something new about him disturbed her, something more than their painful break-up.

When he came around the table toward her then, she took a step backward, wary. The last thing she wanted was for him to touch her or apologize or…whatever he was about to do.

"I'll get the filled boxes for you," he said, indicating the two she'd packed and slid to one side. "They get pretty heavy."

"Oh," she said, feeling silly. "Thanks, but I've still got some muscle." She raised her sweater-clad arm and made a muscle to prove the point.

Rafe was still a little too close, so much so that his outdoorsy scent tinkled her nose. Amy's breath caught in her throat as memories flooded her. Her chest filled with an ache too big to hold. She'd once loved him so very, very much.

Heedless of her inward battle, Rafe's powerful finger

lightly squeezed her relatively small muscle. He whistled. "Spokane girls got the power."

Yes, they did. The power to back away and remember what Rafe Westfield had done five years ago.

She dropped her arm to her side and turned away to rummage in the donation boxes.

They worked in silence again, sorting, stacking, boxing. Amy tried to focus on the good she was doing, on the families who would benefit from the food and toys they'd deliver to homes shortly before Christmas.

"I wish we had a radio," she said suddenly.

"Want to use my iPod? I've got earbuds."

"You downloaded Christmas carols?"

"Are you insinuating that guys don't listen to Christmas music?"

"No, of course not—" Amy looked up to see he was teasing. "How did you know I wanted Christmas music?"

"Because you always did." Expression easy, he pointed a cake mix at her. "You drove me nuts singing 'Jingle Bells' at the first sign of snow."

Not wanting to remember those good times, Amy tossed her head. "Maybe I've changed."

He stared at her for two beats before saying, "I guess we both have. You gonna sing in the Christmas cantata?"

"I hadn't thought about it." But she was thinking about what he'd said. They'd both changed. For some reason, the statement made her sad.

"You should. Trust me, the choir needs your soprano."

"I doubt that." She added packs of beans and rice to the three new boxes she'd set between them as barriers. "New Life has plenty of strong voices."

"None as sweet and pure as yours."

"Is that a compliment?" She looked up, smiling in spite of her resolve.

His perfect mouth shrugged while his eyes twinkled. "Maybe. Or maybe Darlene Clifford is jockeying to sing a solo."

Amy clapped a hand to each cheek. "Argh. Say it ain't so!"

Holding a tea box to his chest, he nodded in mock seriousness. "And we both know Darlene's voice could take the paint off the walls."

Amy sniggered. Then she laughed. Rafe joined her. And in the next minute, through shared silliness, she relaxed a little.

"Shame on you." Amy tossed a bag of noodles at him.

He one-handed it. "You laughed first."

So she had. Rafe could always make her laugh.

But she'd still be glad when the evening was over.

The scream jerked him awake. He bolted upright in bed, shaking, heart thundering inside his chest. The rat-a-tat of gunfire resounded in his head. His nostrils full of fire and dust and that peculiar, sickly sweet smell of death.

Rafe shook his head, fighting to gain reality. He was home. In Snowglobe. In his old bedroom. He'd done his job. Let it go.

He sat up on the side of the bed, elbows on his knees and head in his hands. Cold night air prickled the sweat trickling down his neck.

He could hear his own ragged breathing, loud and harsh in the silent night.

The doorknob rattled and the door opened. Light from the hall bathroom crept in around his feet.

He looked up to find Jake a dark shadow standing in the doorway.

"Are you all right?" Jake asked, voice low and worried.

Rafe ran splayed fingers through the top of his hair, collecting himself for the sake of little brother. "Yeah."

"I heard you."

Shame calmed the pounding of his pulse. Jake's room wa

next to his just as it had always been. Rafe was thankful Mom and Dad were at the other end of the house. But he didn't want his brother thinking he was a sissy. "Sorry."

Jake padded across the soft carpet, quiet as a cat, and a welcome presence. "Another nightmare?"

As much as he hated to admit it.

"Something like that. No big deal. Must have been the chili dog."

Jake hovered, uncertain. "I can get you something. Water. Milk. Ibuprofen."

Rafe wondered if he'd screamed, if he'd cried out like a scared girl. He wondered if he'd said anything he shouldn't. But he didn't ask. Couldn't. He was a marine. "Go back to bed."

"You sure? I could stay. Talk."

"I'm good." He could handle it. "Don't say anything to Mom about this, okay?"

Jake hesitated for another few seconds, then squeezed Rafe's shoulder, slipped quietly out of the room and shut the door with a soft click.

In total darkness again, Rafe sat on the side of the bed, adrenaline jacked, his sleep shot for the night. He couldn't remember details of the dreams but they left him feeling weak and helpless and frustrated that war had followed him home. They didn't come often—maybe once a week—but when they did, they wrecked him.

He bowed his head, hands clasped between his still shaky knees and prayed. Afterward, he rose and went to the window, pulling up the heavy insulated shades to look outside. The world was peaceful here. Peaceful and safe. Snow fell in the moonlight and glistened like the inside of a snowglobe. He thought of the one he'd carried with him all around the world. The snowglobe Amy had given him.

"Amy," he muttered against the cold windowpane.

Tonight had been strange. He'd known she hadn't wanted to be alone with him at the food pantry. Even though he understood her reasons, he was bothered. They'd been such good friends, able to talk about anything and everything, even before becoming engaged. But that, like everything else in his life, had changed.

He wondered again if he should broach the topic of their broken engagement and explain how sorry he was for hurting her.

He scrubbed both hands over his face, whiskers scraping.

He and Amy lived in the same town, attended the same church, but they might as well be as far apart as Spokane and Afghanistan. She hadn't understood then. She certainly wouldn't understand now.

Heart heavy, he clicked on a lamp, went to his closet and took down the small snowglobe. As he had so many times before, he twisted the key on the bottom and gave the globe a shake. He returned to his bed and lay down. Globe balanced on his chest, he propped his hands behind his head to watch the make-believe snow fall over the pretty little village and let the melody of "Silent Night" serenade him toward dawn.

Chapter Four

"What are these things?" Rafe asked, holding up a skewer of meat and fruit.

Jake leaned in and took a bite. Mouth full, he said, "I don't know but they're good. Katie knows how to throw a party, huh?"

The birthday/Christmas party was in full swing, the voices of thirty-plus adults competing with a blasting CD player. Rafe figured there was enough food spread on the table, the bar and the end tables to feed everyone in town for a week, and he aimed to sample all of it. Always a gregarious guy, he was having a good time.

"Hey." Jake's elbow jabbed his ribs. "Look who just walked in."

Rafe knew before he looked. Lots of people had come through the front door tonight but Jake would only mention one. Amy.

"So?" he asked, choking down a cracker covered in spicy cheese spread.

"So, go talk to her. She looks lost."

Rafe made a rude noise. "You should *get* lost."

But he watched Amy step inside, her smile tentative, holding a wrapped gift to add to the pile already stacked a foot high under Katie's twinkling Douglas fir. She did look a little lost as if she'd forgotten how to mingle with old friends.

Before he could consider all the reasons why he shouldn't, he excused his way through the packed room to her side.

At his approach, Amy looked up, startled. "Rafe. I wasn't expecting you."

"Same here." He was glad she'd come. The room seemed brighter, merrier with Amy in it. "You're late."

Amy bent to place her gift beneath the tree. Her blond hair shone like the tinsel and a few stray hairs danced with static electricity. Rafe remembered how soft and smooth her hair was and how he'd liked the feel on his rough fingers.

He remembered a lot of things about Amy that he'd liked. Maybe Jake was right. Maybe they could…

She stood, cutting off the thought he shouldn't be thinking.

"Worked late. Mom had something to do tonight." Her nose was red, her eyes sparkling from the outdoor chill. She looked energized, the way she always had when she'd been outside in the winter. The same way he felt now that she was here.

When she rubbed her reddened hands together, Rafe resisted the urge to warm them as he used to. He wondered if she remembered.

"Let me take your coat," he said, not wanting to let her get away but not knowing what else to say.

"You don't have to." She unsnapped the down anorak and slid it from her shoulders.

Rafe took it anyway. The scent of fresh, frigid air and Amy's warm perfume wafted from the thick jacket. "Cold outside."

Amy gave him a slight smile as if to say, "This is Montana in the winter. Hello! It's always cold," but she didn't say anything. Still, he felt a little schoolboy stupid.

"I'll put this in the back with the others." He was gratified when she followed him through the jostling crowd.

Friends stopped them along the way to say hello, joking, and making merry. Amy hugged Todd, the birthday boy, and teased him about getting old. Rafe had a moment of wishing she'd be that warm and friendly with him, not that he deserved anything except the polite reserve he got.

He didn't know why he couldn't give it up. Guilt, he supposed. He owed her.

"It feels good to be home for Christmas, doesn't it?" he asked when they were alone, just for a minute, in the hallway.

"Yes, it does. What's to eat? I'm starving." She looked back toward the kitchen as if regretting her decision to follow him toward the coat room.

"No time for dinner?"

"No. This is the busy season."

He tossed the coat on Katie's bed with a stack of others and steered her back through the crush. "I highly recommend those kabob things and the hot cheese dip and the pizza and those whirly pinwheel things over there."

Amy's eyes widened. "You tried all those?"

"Just getting started, too. What's your pleasure?" He handed her a red paper plate decorated with a smiling reindeer. "There's dessert but you need sustenance first."

"Sustenance. Good word. How about the fruit dip and some of those veggies?"

"Girl food, but okay. Beats MREs." Rafe popped a cookie in his mouth, having a better time than he'd expected. At least Amy was talking to him. She was cool but conversant.

The need to discuss the past pushed in. He pushed back. *Don't mess up the moment.* This time last year he'd been lying in a dirt sleeping hole in the barren outposts of Afghanistan. He'd daydreamed of home, of Christmas parties like this, of good friends and good times, and if Amy occupied a lot of those dreams, it was only natural. They'd been together since junior high.

"Amy. Rafe." Katie appeared next to them. "This is awesome. I wasn't sure you'd both come, but seeing you together again just makes my day."

Amy made some light remark before Katie moved on, but Rafe felt her withdrawal. She went from friendly Amy to a stiff stranger who quickly wandered away. And Rafe was left out in the cold.

The party was great. The food was delicious. The Dirty Santa game hilarious. Watching grown men finagle and fuss over a pair of snow goggles proved to be the hit of the night. Amy was having fun. Truly. She'd reconnected with her high school friends, including Mack Jennings, who showed more than a passing interest in her homecoming.

"I'm going for more punch," Mack, standing at her elbow, said. "Want some?"

"Sure, if you don't mind."

With a wink, he took her cup and disappeared through the crush. She took an olive from a tray and swiveled around on the bar stool. The first person she spotted was Rafe. She started to turn away but curiosity got the better of her. He hadn't seemed the least bothered by her avoidance of him. That was good, she supposed. They were both going on with their lives, dealing with the past the way mature adults should.

Katie's comment, her insinuation that Rafe and Amy were *together,* had bothered her. So much so that she'd slipped away from Rafe at the first opportunity. No matter what well-meaning friends thought, painful experience had taught her to protect her heart. Sure, Rafe was the hometown hero, the nice guy who delivered food baskets and taught disabled kids to ski, but that didn't make him trustworthy.

She watched him now, sitting across the big living room in an armchair sharing laughs with his brother and Gabby Ralick. The Westfield brothers, in her opinion, were the best-looking men in the room, and Gabby, a divorcée with two kids, seemed to be thrilled with the attention.

Mack returned with her refilled cup of punch and slid onto the stool next to her. "It's not polite to stare."

Amy lowered her gaze to the paper cup and nonchalantly sipped the sweet liquid. "I wasn't staring."

"He was."

"No, he wasn't! Why would he be?"

"Maybe he still has a thing for you."

"I certainly hope not," she said hotly, but a flutter of… something…stirred beneath her rib cage.

Mack lifted his cup in a toast. "I'll drink to that."

They bumped cups.

"The clinic is having a party next Wednesday afternoon. Want to come over and hang out with us medical types?"

The invitation caught Amy off guard. Mack was a radiology tech at the local medical clinic, and she knew practically everyone else who worked there, too. At least, she used to know them. While she was considering her reply, the growl of Katie and Todd's karaoke machine interrupted.

"Karaoke Christmas, everyone!" Todd shouted into the microphone, which caused a feedback squeal that killed any notion of conversation.

Amy pressed her hands to both ears, laughing.

Todd kicked off the karaoke by *barking* a hilarious rendition of "Jingle Bells," and others followed, singing the silliest holiday tunes they could find. Mack brought the house down when he sang "I Want a Hippopotamus for Christmas" in a girly soprano, and not to be outdone, Jake warbled and acted out "Randolph, the Bowlegged Cowboy."

When he finished and the stomps and claps subsided, Jake shot an ornery grin toward Amy and then toward his brother. Amy got a funny feeling in her stomach and slid down on the bar stool.

"Who wants to hear Rafe and Amy sing?" Jake shouted. "Just like old times. A duet."

Amy's gaze flew toward Rafe, who had the same deer-in-the-headlights expression she suspected was on her own face. But unlike Amy, Rafe unwound his tall form from the armchair, shedding Gabby as he came toward the front of the room and the karaoke machine.

"How about it, Amy?" Jake called, urging her on, his grin so annoying she wanted to pinch him. "Come on, now, don't be shy. Amy. Amy."

The crowd picked up the chant. "Amy. Amy."

As much as she didn't want to sing "their" duet, the situation was getting embarrassing.

She shot a frantic look at Mack, who hitched his chin toward the front. "Might as well get it over with."

Gulping down panic, Amy headed to the front amidst good-natured catcalls and whistles. If any of these so-called friends recalled the history between Rafe and Amy, they'd been struck with a sudden case of group amnesia.

Or maybe that's why they were so insistent.

Well, she'd show them. She could sing with anyone. But she would not sing *their* song.

She'd no more than thought the thought than Todd slipped a CD into the karaoke machine and the music started. She looked at Rafe in panic.

"No," she whispered.

"Don't make a big deal of it." He squeezed her hand. "It's just a song."

Just a song? Did he know how much that hurt?

And when had he taken hold of her hand?

He smiled into her eyes.

"I don't even like you," she whispered.

His lips curved upward. "I know."

Then the intro ended and Rafe began to sing the first verse of "All I Want for Christmas is You."

Amy had sung for events since she was a tot. Singing didn't scare her. But she didn't want anyone in this room to think she still pined for Rafe Westfield.

She whirled around and grabbed Jake by the collar, crooning her first two lines into his surprised face.

Then she spun toward Todd and grabbed him, proclaiming that he could make her wish come true.

"Hey!" Katie hollered, pretending insult. "He's taken. Except for when he snores."

The room erupted in laughter and Amy relaxed. They were singing silly songs and she'd made this one fit the theme.

Todd took her hand and gave her a spin, turning her back toward Rafe. She stumbled in the spin and he caught her, reeled her in and stared down into her face as he sang of wanting to hold her tight.

Putting on an act for the crowd, he hugged her close in mock affection, but Amy felt the rattle of his heart through his shirt. He was as embarrassed by the attention as she was and probably wished he hadn't come to the party. He probably wished she'd stayed in Spokane.

An urge to snuggle into his broad chest and listen to his strong baritone troubled her. He smelled good, like the woods in spring, and she felt so secure in his arms.

She stiffened, remembering. She was not secure with Rafe, war hero or not. She could not trust him, never could, though she'd been foolish enough to believe for a while.

She backed away, fanning herself, playing the game, giving their friends a good laugh as she and Rafe finished the performance with a dramatic flourish.

Amy hoped no one noticed that her smile was a little too tight.

Rafe leaned into her ear and whispered, "Sorry to put you on the spot. You okay?"

She nodded, face frozen in a fake smile. Of course she was okay, even if she felt like crying.

Chapter Five

Amy thought about the Christmas party for days afterward, and each time she and Rafe ran into each other—an inevitability in Snowglobe—she was reminded again of that one tiny moment. The moment he'd pulled her close, even in jest, she'd flashed back to those perfect days of feeling secure in his love.

She rang up a customer's purchase, a set of keepsake ornaments.

"No time for a cup of hot cider?" she asked the woman, a teacher at the elementary school.

"Not today, Amy. We have a family gathering tonight to decorate the tree. I still need to put on a ham and bake a pie."

"Sounds fun." Smiling, she handed the woman her bag. "Enjoy. And Merry Christmas!"

The jingle bells on the door wreath jangled merrily as the customer departed. Her mom, who looked especially pretty in a bright blue top with a flowy jacket, came from the back of the shop where she'd been unpacking today's shipment of gift items.

"Are you working at the church tonight?"

"That's the plan," Amy said, nonchalantly. "How about you?"

Dana shook her head, dark hair swinging like something

out of a shampoo commercial. "Not tonight. I have other plans."

Before Amy could ask what those plans might be, her mom rushed on. "Why don't you go ahead and leave? You'll need to eat first anyway. I'll close up and see you at home later tonight. Okay?"

Amy blinked, noticing the sudden bloom of color on her mother's cheeks. Was her mom trying to get rid of her?

"Are you sure? I don't mind staying. Rafe has plenty of help scheduled tonight. I saw the list myself."

Mom's hands stilled on a display of glossy gold wrapping paper. "How is that working out? You and Rafe?"

"If you mean, are we civil, the answer is yes." She got her purse from beneath the counter.

"I heard you had fun together at Katie's party."

"Really? You heard that?"

"Did you?"

Had she? "Jake put us in an embarrassing spot. He forced us to sing a duet."

"The two of you always sounded good together. Your sweet soprano and his strong baritone."

She didn't appreciate reminders of Rafe's baritone crooning a love song in her ear. "We survived."

"Mmm," Mom said. "I heard there were sparks. That Rafe couldn't take his eyes off you all night."

Amy's heart jumped. Was that even the slightest bit true? "Come on, Mother. You can't want us to get back together."

"I would never interfere in your life." Her mom grinned. "Not much anyway. But Rafe is a good man who lives his faith. I want that for my child, a man who loves God with everything he has. Faith matters, baby."

Amy heard what her mother would never say. Amy's dad had attended church on special occasions, but he'd never really served God. He'd never really loved his wife and daughter, either. If he had, he wouldn't have walked out on them.

"I'll find a Christian guy. Don't worry, Mom."

Dana gave her a quick hug. "I just want you to be happy."

"I am." Most of the time. She'd love to settle down and have a family, but God would send her someone. She hoped.

After slipping into her coat, she headed to her car, her mother's words ringing in her head. Rafe was a good man. He was. He always had been, but his faith had been wobbly back then. Since coming home she'd seen how he'd thrown himself into the town, into the church, into his business, into the needs of others. He'd matured.

Okay, so she appreciated the man he appeared to have become, but she knew better than most that appearances could be deceiving.

The church family hall was crowded on this particular night, but Rafe knew the minute Amy arrived. The truth troubled him. Any time Amy was anywhere in the vicinity, he felt her presence. He'd thought he was over her, but the more he saw her, the more he wondered. She was a reminder of his failures as a man, but she also reminded him of what it had been like to be crazy in love. He'd never come close to that feeling with any other woman.

He'd prayed about it lately. Almost as much as he prayed about the bad dreams. Apparently, God wanted him to notice her. Maybe the Lord was pushing him to bring up the past, set it to rights. He certainly thought about it often enough, just as he thought about her.

She came toward him, shedding her coat, and he let himself enjoy the sight. Vibrant, glowing with health and energy, Amy made him appreciate the differences in male and female.

"What's my assignment, Chief?" she asked.

"Early deliveries start tomorrow. Since you're our premiere

basket wrapper, why don't you show some of the other ladies how to fancy up the finished boxes with those bow thingies your mom donated."

"Works for me. Should we wrap the toys, too, or leave those for the parents to wrap?"

"Leave them. We'll include gift wrap in the boxes. Your mother donated that, too."

"Great lady, my mom." Amy moved away to do his bidding and gathered a group of women around a table. In minutes, colored ribbon became fancy bows and boxes became pretty gift packages. The lady had a knack for making things beautiful.

Busy sorting and directing and keeping an eye on all phases of the operation, Rafe could work anywhere he chose. And he chose to work near Amy. He directed conversation her way and was gratified when she didn't freeze him out. The talk turned from the Christmas tree lighting and the annual church drama to the amount of snow on the ski slopes.

"Have you been skiing yet?" he asked, pretending the question was casual conversation for all, though he directed it at Amy. There were at least twenty other people in the room, most of them asking him questions from time to time, and yet he kept returning to Amy.

Something was going on here, whether he liked it or not.

"I've been too busy with the shop," Amy said as she wound ribbon around her outstretched fingers to deftly, quickly create a glittering bow. "Mom wants to go part-time after the holidays so I'm in a time crunch to learn everything."

She zipped the edge of her scissors along the dangling length of red and silver ribbon. The strips curled into long ringlets around the central bow.

"You've worked in that shop all your life."

"But Mom did all the ordering, dealt with vendors and billing. I know how. I just have to learn the nuances."

"Ah, those pesky nuances," he said wryly and handed her a roll of cellophane tape.

She laughed and the sound pleased him, warming him like a mug of hot chocolate after a fast ride on the Arctic Cat.

"How's the sports rental business? Jake says you're making a killing."

She ripped off a strip of tape and handed him the dispenser. He laid it aside and went back to checking his list. When had she talked to Jake? And why? Was his brother up to something?

"The ski race brings in a lot of tourists," he said. "Tourists want to have fun. The Westfield brothers are the kings of fun."

Amy's eyes puckered in amusement. "Who knew the two of us could become regular entrepreneurs?"

"We've always had a lot in common."

Her smile faded. "Yeah, well…" She fluffed an already fluffy bow and then scooted a box marked with a name and address to one side. "This family is really far from town. Who's doing the deliveries on the distant homes?"

He wasn't sure what he'd said to upset her, but he wanted her smile back. "Don't know yet. No one's signed up for the outer limits yet."

"I will."

"You'll have to take a snowmobile to most of these places." He tapped a finger on the cardboard box. "Crick Pass is impassable in any other vehicle this time of year."

She cocked her head to one side, eyes twinkling. "Then why do they call it a pass?"

Ah, there she was, the real Amy, the girl who loved to have fun. Suddenly, he felt better.

"Come on. The list of addresses is in the office. Let's go map out the houses we can only reach by snowmobile."

"You gonna let me take one of your fancy new rides? Or do I have to drive Mom's old sled?"

"Is that thing still running?"

"Most of the time."

"I think you better try out Jake's new Arctic Cat. It's a sweet machine."

"Sounds like a plan." She moved away from the table toward the office in the back of the Family Center. "You have GPS?"

"On everything we rent now."

"Good. Map out the route, and I'll dress up in my elf suit and start delivering tomorrow afternoon."

Rafe stopped in his tracks. "You have an elf suit?"

Her eyebrows wiggled playfully. "Doesn't everyone?"

Then she did something the old Amy would have done. She bumped him in the side with her shoulder and giggled.

The next afternoon the air was so still Amy could hear the ground snow crackle like breakfast cereal. She blew out her breath, a frosty cloud, though she was so heavily attired she'd probably be sweating shortly.

She pushed open the door to Westfield Sports Rentals and stepped inside the warm warehouselike structure. Loud rock music jarred the space. It was her first visit to Rafe's business and she took in the orderly rows of equipment, the well-swept concrete floor, the waiting area. A couple of round tables with chairs encouraged customers to relax, and on a table against one wall, a pot sent up the fragrance of good-quality coffee.

Jake, busy outfitting a family with snowboards, lifted a hand to wave. She wiggled her fingers at him.

"Rafe's out back, getting the sleds ready."

"Okay. Thanks." She followed the direction of his point, through a metal door that led outside.

"There you are," he said, looking up with that welcoming smile and those new lines around his eyes she found particularly attractive. "Ready?"

Looking at the line of snowmobiles, ready and waiting for a rider, Amy asked, "Which one do I take?"

"You choose. I'll ride one of these with the passenger sleigh on back to haul the food baskets." He patted the fender of a big blue machine connected to an oval-shaped enclosure on skids.

She noticed then that he was geared up for the weather. "You're going?"

His too-serious eyes squinted. "Wasn't that the plan?"

Amy blinked. Had it been? "I thought I was going alone."

"Not going to happen. Too dangerous."

Her hackles went up. "I've been riding these mountains all my life. I'm perfectly capable."

"I didn't say you weren't. I just don't think it's a good idea for you to go alone."

Her grip tightened on the handlebar of the machine. "I can make that decision for myself."

He looked as though he wanted to argue but refrained. The tension between them crackled. Hands on his hips, Rafe looked off toward the snow-covered mountains for several long seconds. When his focus came back to her, his annoyance was gone.

Gently, with just a touch of humor, he chided, "What are you trying to do, Ames? Hog up all the blessings for yourself?"

Ames. No one had called her Ames in a long, long time. She opened her mouth to argue but the words didn't come. He'd worked harder on this project than she had, and delivering *was* the greatest blessing and the most fun.

An array of emotions shifted through her. An afternoon alone in the wilderness with Rafe?

She mounted the snowmobile and started the engine. "Just try to keep up."

A slow grin slid over his handsome features. "You're on, Ames. You're on."

Chapter Six

"He's thinking of selling out next spring," Rafe said as he and Amy left the last of the remote homes, a forlorn-looking ranch house with smoke spiraling from the chimney. "Economic times are hard enough and now winter's taken a toll on his animals."

"It must be incredibly hard for him to ranch and care for three kids since his wife died."

While Rafe had talked with the rancher and warmed himself by the woodstove Amy had played with the motherless baby. Her heart ached for the man and his children.

"He seemed pretty down—embarrassed, too." Vapor clouds puffed from his lips like smoke rings. "A real man doesn't like taking charity, but he wanted his kids to have Christmas."

"I'm so sad for all of them. I wish I knew some other way to help. The ranch is so far out here, he can't have many visitors."

"The life of a Montana rancher." Rafe pulled his helmet into place and mounted the snowmobile.

"I suppose." Still, she wanted to do more. The smiles and gratitude of the other families had blessed her, but the proud rancher and his kids tugged at her heart. "It was nice of you to offer to come up and drive them to the church drama."

He shrugged a thickly clad shoulder, the silky material whispering. "I have the equipment. Not a big deal."

"It was to them." She spun the snowmobile around and started back along the tracks they'd made coming in, thinking. About her blessings. About the rancher's plight. About Rafe.

They rode for a mile or two, road wind flapping around them, snow spitting up from the ground. After a bit, Rafe gunned his engine and passed her, lifting one gloved hand to point behind him. She got his message. He could beat her even pulling a passenger sled. Challenged, Amy caught up and returned the favor, mood elevated a little to play in the great Montana outdoors with Rafe.

Miles and miles of pristine snow frosted the meadows and forests. In places, drifts many feet high stacked against the cliffs and mountains. They'd carved a route on their way up but even now, snow flew around them like a blizzard until her vision was obscured. It was a wonderland of beauty and treachery.

As they neared the outskirts of Snowglobe, the land flattened into an area sparsely populated. In the powder bowl ahead, the amber lights of town and home glowed like angel halos. Rafe pulled alongside her and motioned for her to stop.

Curious, Amy followed his lead and drove across a bumpy thicket of snow, through a scattering of tall pines toward… nothing. An empty snowy meadow. Rafe stopped and killed his engine, straddling the snowmobile.

Amy pulled up next to him and flipped up her visor. "Why are we stopping?"

Rafe ripped off his helmet and speared her with an incomprehensible look, gaze as gray and intense as the sky above. "Wanted to show you something."

Amy parked her ride and dismounted, the rumble of the machine still humming through her muscles though she'd shut down the engine.

Rafe came up beside her. "Look around at this place. What do you think?"

She looked at him first, saw an eager hope and knew he was showing her something important. Taking her time, she turned slowly, gazing over the ripples and hills of snow, taking in the mountain backdrop, the forest, the panorama of sky above and valley below.

"In spring a creek runs along the back," he said, pointing, "through that line of trees and down toward the valley. The land is fairly flat here, plenty of space."

And then she knew. A lump formed in her throat. "You bought it."

"Next spring, if all goes well, I'll start building."

They'd once talked about building their own little paradise in the mountains. Now Rafe was going ahead with their dreams. A moment of sadness at all they'd lost came and went, and then she was glad for him.

"You deserve to have a wonderful place."

"Mom and Dad have been great since I got home, but it's time I moved out."

"This will be perfect."

As if he'd been awaiting her approval, Rafe eagerly launched into the plans.

"What do you think about putting the house right here?"

"Facing the valley or the mountains?"

He stopped, frowning. "Good question."

"I know," she said. "Do both. Build a house with incredible views open to both sides. Lots of tall windows, a double deck."

"Skylights." His smile widened. He raised both arms, fists clenched in a victory punch, reminding her of a little boy at

Christmas. "Ames, you're a genius. Will you help me with the plans? I need your artistic eye."

The compliment sizzled along her nerve endings and she caught his excitement. "How many square feet?"

"Flexible."

"Cathedral ceilings or two-story?"

"Yes."

She laughed and the sound puffed out in a noisy, foggy cloud that startled the birds from a nearby pine. She laughed again. "Tell me what you have in mind. This is exciting."

Rafe's quick description included an enormous beamed living room with a full wall fireplace and a game room. "It's the kitchen and all that stuff I have trouble with. I mean, how much room does a man need for a microwave?"

Amy thumped a gloved hand against his thickly coated arm. "Goofy. An incredible kitchen is *everything*. Even if you don't cook a lot, you'll want a beautiful space, just in case." *Just in case you get married. Just in case you fall in love.* The idea of Rafe and another woman pinched, but she let it go, clasping the pleasure of the moment. "Lots of gleaming wood, granite, a center island that opens up the whole living/dining area."

Rafe grinned and looped an elbow around her neck, snugging her close to his side. "See why I need you? You're brilliant."

"Well, of course I am. I am *woman*."

She'd meant the statement as a joke, but Rafe's expression went serious as he gazed down into her face. "Yes, you are. And quite a woman, at that."

Her grin softened to a smile, a mere curve of lips, as she gazed back at him. They were different people now. Grownups. She could spend this time with him, enjoy his company, throw herself into planning his dream home. After all, she *had* forgiven him even if she hadn't forgotten.

The quiet of the day, broken only by the crackle of frozen earth and the occasional cry of a bird surrounded them in a cocoon of winter wonderland. Rafe's warmth seeped through his jacket into hers, his arm feeling right and good around her. Without thinking too much, a nasty habit of hers, she circled his lean waist with one arm and leaned against his solid bulk.

He hugged her closer until his chin rested on her hair. "Ames?" he said.

Her pulse thudded in her throat. "What?"

A second passed and then two while she wondered what he was about to say, and wondered even more if she wanted to hear it. Something was stirring inside her again for Rafe Westfield. Maybe Mom was right.

She licked suddenly dry lips and lifted her chin. "You were saying?"

Rafe stared out across the clearing for another second before saying, "Nothing important."

Slight disappointment tugged at her. "Oh."

She started to pull away but Rafe pulled her back. "On second thought, I *was* about to say something."

Her heart bumped. "Which was?"

"The Chamber is offering sleigh rides after the tree lighting. Want to come along? Maybe lead the kids in some Christmas carols?"

She studied his face, certain he'd had something else in mind. But even this sounded too close, too personal, too scary. "Are you driving the sleigh for the foster kids?"

"Yep. Just like always."

"Santa Rafe." *Don't do it,* her brain yelled. *Don't do it.*

He grinned. "I like that. Will you come?"

Ignoring the inner sentries she'd erected against this particular man, she said, "I'd love it."

He kissed the top of her head. "Afterward, if it's not too

late, I'll ply you with pizza and show you my fledgling house designs. How does that sound?"

A lot better than it should.

On the ride home, they'd raced, thrown snow on each other and laughed like loons. All the while the feel of Rafe's casual kiss on the head warmed a place long empty inside of Amy. Though she was unsure of what it meant, a new relationship was slowly developing. She didn't know how she felt about it, but Rafe was clearly an unresolved issue or she wouldn't think about him so much.

Perhaps this was the answer to her prayers, a chance to resolve the past and move forward, one way or the other. It was the other that made her nervous.

After they'd parked the snowmobiles and warmed up, Rafe walked her to her car. He opened the door, waited until she was inside and closed it, motioning for her to roll down the window. He leaned in as she cranked the engine. "Thanks for sharing the blessings. I enjoyed it."

"Me, too."

He did the quiet thing again, staring at her as if something heavy plagued his mind. Finally, he cupped her cheek with a gloved hand and smiled, then slapped the window opening with a single pop and backed away. "Be safe."

Night closed in as Amy headed for home through the cheery lighted town, her insides glowing like the lights of Snowglobe. The snowplow had scraped the narrow streets during her absence, a constant in the tiny town. Thoughts of Rafe and the afternoon, of the rancher and his mother-less kids, and of the dream home Rafe would build filled her head. He was eager, it seemed, to move on with life after the military, a revelation that had caused her opinion to shift a little. She'd never asked him why he'd given up the career he'd claimed to want more than marriage to her. He'd come home to Snowglobe, just as she had. And he was putting down roots. Building a home. Making a life. She knew he wasn't seeing anyone special, but a man didn't build a house to live in it alone. Did he?

If Rafe found someone else, would she mind?

The answer was yes. Even with their painful parting years ago, she still had feelings for Rafe Westfield.

A thought both elated and scared her. Could she let go and see where this tangle of feelings might take her? Did she dare trust him again?

As she pulled into her mother's drive, she noticed an unfamiliar truck parked outside. Her mom had company. Probably one of the ladies from the Bible study or the hospital auxiliary. Dana was on so many committees, the visitor could be anyone in town.

Amy bounded up the steps eager for the warmth inside the cozy house. She pushed open the door and stepped in. Her first impressions were of the recently hung garlands festooning the living room and the spicy scent of Mexican casserole. She followed the scent toward the kitchen, expecting to find her mother.

She rounded the door frame and blinked in confusion. A man carried a casserole dish toward the glass-topped table while her mother filled two coffee cups.

"Amy! I didn't hear you come in." Dana's olive skin flushed beneath dark eyes that sparkled with an energy Amy had never observed before.

What was going on here?

"Honey, I want you to meet Jeffrey Fischer." Looking flustered, her mom set the cups on the table and looped elbows with the man. He was blond, like Dad, with piercing blue eyes. Amy's stomach twisted at the thought of her long-absent, uncaring father. "He bought the old Cleveland house and moved up from Helena last spring."

"Hi." Amy nodded toward the newcomer. "Nice to meet you." *Sort of. What are you doing here with my mother?*

Jeffrey reached out and shook her hand. Then he slid an arm around her mom and smiled into Dana's face with an expression of affection. "Your mother's told me so much about you."

Wish I could say the same about you. But Amy found her manners in time to say with humor, "Don't believe a word of it. I'm not that bad."

"I'm sorry the two of you haven't met before. I was waiting for the right time." Again, Mom seemed flustered as though worried about Amy's approval. "I thought we might all have Christmas dinner, spend the day together. Jeffrey has a daughter in California who may come for a visit. Her name is Lisa. You'll like her. Very sweet young woman."

Dana Caldwell was not one to prattle on nervously. The fact that she did raised Amy's suspicion that Jeffrey was more than a casual acquaintance.

"Correct me if I'm wrong, sweetie," Jeffrey said to Dana with a tender look. "But what I think you're trying to say is that we've been spending a lot of time together and we hope to spend more." To Amy he said, "Your mother is an amazing woman. The day I stumbled into her shop to order flowers for Lisa's birthday was one of the best days of my life."

"And the rest, as they say, is history," Dana said with an airy flutter of fingers.

Stunned realization slid down Amy's back. Whoa. Mom had a boyfriend? When had this happened?

Amy looked from Jeffrey's face to her mother's and back again. This man was in love with her mother. And maybe her mom felt the same.

The sudden paradigm shift was too much for Amy to take in. Silly as it was, she felt alone and left out, an unwanted intruder. "Don't let me interrupt your dinner. You two go ahead."

"Why don't you join us, honey? There's plenty. Jeffrey brought his special Mexican chicken dish."

"Makes enough to feed an army," Jeffrey said. "Afterward, we'll finish decorating the tree and watch *It's a Wonderful Life.*"

Mom's favorite movie. Amy's, too. Watching it together was their tradition.

Amy managed a weak smile. "I'm pretty tired. I think I'll head off to my room and a hot bath. Warm up after the afternoon on a snowmobile."

If she expected her mother to argue, she was wrong. Confused and a little hurt, Amy left the kitchen. Her mother had a boyfriend. She wasn't surprised that a nice man would find Dana attractive. Mom was gorgeous and smart and successful. But since Amy's father walked out, Dana had never dated anyone. Not that Amy knew about. Mom's desire to retire and "kick up her heels" suddenly made a lot more sense.

Just as suddenly Amy felt as intrusive as the proverbial fifth wheel. She should be glad for her mother. She knew that. Rationally she was. Dana deserved something besides work and charitable deeds, but try as she might, Amy felt adrift and lonely, like a windsock dangling from a pole. Exactly the way she'd felt when Dad left. And again when Rafe had joined the marines.

Alone in her bedroom, Amy hung up her coat and sat on the side of the bed. Her heart thudded against her chest.

"Lord, I'm confused," she murmured. "I want to get over myself. I want to be happy for Mom. I want to get over Rafe."

There it was. The deep wound that wouldn't heal. She'd never gotten over the heartbreak of losing Rafe no matter where she went or what she did. Tonight, seeing her mom with a man, happy and fluttery and falling in love, brought the issue to a head.

She wanted what her mother had found, but she was too scared of getting hurt again to do anything about it.

Chapter Seven

The song "Let it Snow! Let it Snow! Let it Snow!" drifted from the shop's piped-in music as Amy locked up for the night.

"Appropriate," she muttered with a glance out at the heavy snow falling on the nearly abandoned streets. The wind had picked up, along with the snow, and the meteorologist said they were in for a storm. Across the street, Hank Redford battled the wind, head down, as he hurried from his pharmacy to his car. They might be in for another blizzard.

Going to the back, she emptied and washed the urn, sealed the leftover pumpkin cookies, and tidied up. The last customer had come and gone, along with her mother who'd gone off to Kalispell hours ago with Jeffrey. A little worry niggled and Amy prayed they'd have a safe return.

As she moved toward the front, turning off little trees and fragrance burners as she went, she heard a sound above the wind. *Scratch. Scratch. Scratch.* She cocked her head, eyes squinted to listen. Not tree limbs. There were no trees near enough.

Curious, Amy rounded the sales counter to find a sad-faced dog staring at her through the front door glass. "You poor thing. You're shivering."

Though Mom would not take kindly to a large dog inside the shop of delicate merchandise, Amy's tender heart got the better of her. She opened the door. Wind and snow whipped inside so fast it took Amy's breath. She shivered, too.

The dog waited for no invitation. She rushed inside and shook herself.

Snow sprayed Amy's clothes and sprinkled the tile floor with wet drops. "You're going to get us both in a lot of trouble. Sit."

To her surprise, the dog plopped down on her bottom. She was a large mixed breed, brindle brown with floppy ears and expressive liquid eyes that stared desperately at Amy. In a second, she was up again, pacing in circles, her sides heaving. Amy saw the problem. The dog was pregnant. Very pregnant.

Amy rushed to the back for a towel. When she returned the dog was behind the counter, scratching scattered pieces of wrapping paper into one spot.

"Good thing I haven't swept yet. You're making a bed, aren't you, girl? And not a very comfy one." Amy added the towel atop the wadded papers and then went back for a few more, along with a roll of paper towels, a plastic cup of water and the pumpkin cookies. The poor dog looked hungry and cold and about to deliver puppies.

"What's your name, mama?" Amy asked. "Do you have a home? Where's your owner and what are you doing out on a night like this?"

Amy figured she knew. With no collar and as thin as she was above the bulging belly, the dog was likely a stray. Even in Snowglobe, dogs were abandoned or sometimes wandered away from home, never to be reclaimed.

The dog circled once more and then collapsed with a sigh. Amy sat down on the floor next to her and stroked the wide forehead and velvety ears. "What am I going to do with you, girl? I can't stay here all night, and neither can you."

The dog propped her chin on Amy's knee and lifted sad brown eyes. Tenderness sprang up inside Amy. "Poor thing. Don't worry. I won't throw you out in the cold."

As if she understood, the mama dog sighed again and then got down to the hard work of giving birth.

Rafe noticed the lights burning inside The Snowglobe Gift Shoppe the moment he turned onto Main Street. A glance at the clock on his dash confirmed what he already knew. It was eight o'clock, long past closing time, and with the storm blowing in, Amy and Dana should be safely home.

Through the flop and scrape of overworked windshield wipers, he noted the light burning in Porter's Bakery, too. That was normal. Becka kept late hours and early mornings, especially during the holiday season.

Just to be sure, he stopped there first, and after confirming that all was well, continued to The Snowglobe Gift Shoppe.

Huddled inside his coat against the frigid wind, he pounded at the locked door. "Amy. Dana."

Through the glass he saw Amy come around from the back of the counter. She unclicked the dead bolt to let him in.

"Rafe, what are you doing here?" She shut the door behind him but not before cold circled in, stealing some of the shop's warmth. "The weather is awful. You shouldn't be out."

"I was thinking the same about you." He stomped his feet on the cheery Christmas mat and brushed the quickly melting snow from his coat. "Saw your light. Wanted to be sure you and Dana are okay."

"I'm minding the store today. Mom's out with her new boyfriend."

He was glad he'd stopped. Yesterday, after he'd showed her the building site, he'd gotten the impression she wasn't angry with him anymore. That maybe…well, he'd been hopeful.

"So Dana finally told you about Jeffrey."

"You knew?"

"They've been seeing each other for a while. Dana was worried about your reaction."

"I'm fine with it. He seems nice."

By her clipped tone he realized the new relationship bothered her more than she wanted to admit.

"He's a good guy, Ames. Give him a chance."

"I will. It's just that…" she shrugged.

Rafe finished for her. "It seems weird for your mom to have a boyfriend?"

"Exactly. And I feel kind of—" She pressed a finger and thumb to her temples. "Never mind. Juvenile reaction. I need to shut up."

"You don't need to worry about Jeffrey, if that's what you're thinking. Not that he deserves someone as terrific as your mom."

Some of the tension left her face as she teased. "You've always been half in love with my mother."

"What do you mean, half?"

They both laughed and Rafe relaxed. Dana had been a second mother to him for as long as he and Amy had been an item. Even after the break-up, she'd gone out of her way to show kindness. He still had the letters Dana and the church ladies had written him in Afghanistan, the ones that kept him too aware of Amy and her life in Spokane.

"So what are you doing here this late?" he asked. "Afraid to drive home in the storm?"

"Please." She scoffed. "I was born in Montana. I am not afraid of a snowstorm. Come here and I'll show you what's keeping me."

"Wrapping gifts this late?" he quipped. "What did you buy me? Hope it's not a necktie." To make her laugh, he stuck a crooked finger to his throat and made a choking noise.

"Ha-ha. Very funny." She motioned toward the counter

and he followed, glad to see her smiling at his joke. She was definitely warming up to him. "I had a visitor who doesn't want to leave."

Rafe's hackles rose. Someone was giving Amy trouble? "Who?"

He must have looked fierce because Amy patted his arm. "No need to whip out your commando gear. It isn't a who. Not exactly."

The smell of wet dog assailed him before he spotted the brownish animal curved on its side.

"She arrived just as I was locking up," Amy said. "She looked so pitiful and cold, I brought her in."

The dog paid them no mind as her sides heaved.

"She's having puppies."

"Looks that way."

Rafe hunkered down next to the animal and stroked her ears. "Hey, old girl. Rough night?" To Amy he said, "What are you going to do with her?"

"I don't know, but I can't throw her out."

At that moment, the dog heaved again and delivered a tiny puppy.

"Oh." Amy's breathy gasp had Rafe watching her face. "Rafe, look."

"I'm looking." *At you. At the tenderness in your eyes, the kindness I fell in love with, the wonder we share at the beauty of God's creation.*

She clasped her hands below her chin in a kind of excited prayer. "Here comes another."

Rafe tugged her down to the floor where they sat cross-legged and watched in silence as four puppies were born. Though weary, the mother dog stayed busy, nuzzling and cleaning and urging the squirming babies to nourishment.

It was special, Rafe thought, to sit here on chilly tile with Amy and share this moment. Only a few lights, mostly of th village in the display window and the bulb over the counter, remained on. Music from Dana's stereo played in the background, an Amy Grant song he recognized, "Breath of Heaven."

"Know what this reminds me of?" he asked, voice hushed.

"What?" She turned her face his direction and his pulse leaped. Foolish thing.

"A long ago night in Bethlehem when a very young woman had no place to have her baby."

"Oh, Rafe." She touched his knee. "What a lovely thought. Right here at Christmas." She glanced back at the dog. "No room at the inn."

"Imagine that night, how scary the situation must have been for Mary and Joseph. Away from home and family, not knowing anyone, unable to find shelter."

"And she was in labor."

Rafe took hold of her hand, rewarded when she didn't pull away. "They still use caves as shelter in the Middle East, particularly for animals."

"I didn't know that."

He fiddled with her fingers, lifting each one, loving the feel of her small softness. "I thought about those things a lot when I was there. About how the most special baby ever born had such humble beginnings."

"King of kings," she whispered. "Born in a stable with only rags for a blanket."

"And two people who believed in God's word against all odds." He shifted toward her, intuitively rubbing her third finger where his ring had once resided. It was Amy on his mind, Amy in his constant thoughts. Was God giving them a second chance?

"The Bible makes their choices seem easy, but they couldn't have been, not in that society, not ever."

Some choices were never easy. Not his decision to join

the marines, not the decision to come home. He'd made the right choice to protect his country, but sometimes he wondered about the rest. Would Amy ever understand that he'd thought he was doing the right thing for her? That, even now, he wondered if he was being fair to her? Was it right to restart a relationship when the weakness he'd brought home from the war still lingered?

"I'd like to have their kind of faith," he said. "Being there, in the Middle East, changed me, made God more real."

Amy curled her fingers into his. "I've noticed."

She had? He searched her face, wondering. In the past, they'd never talked much about faith.

"When I was a kid, the Christmas story was kind of a fairy tale to me, something that happened long ago and far away or maybe not at all."

"What changed you?" She was serious, the amber eyes seeking. Did Amy struggle, as he did, with questions no one could answer?

He wondered what she'd say if he told her about the nightmares, about her little snowglobe that helped him sleep when the dreams wouldn't. He didn't, of course. A marine didn't whine.

"Lots of things," he said, gently massaging her palm with his thumb. "Mostly, Him. A man can spend a lot of time praying and listening in a place like that."

"You're different," she said, a statement that neither judged nor accepted.

The soft rooting sounds of newborn puppies drew their attention back to the sweet scene of mother and babies. He didn't release her hand and though her fingers relaxed, she didn't tug them free.

A pulse beat of tenderness thrummed in his chest, both for the animals and for the woman.

What would Amy say if he told her of his feelings? Tha

he wanted another chance to make things right? In recent days they'd formed a fledgling friendship, a new beginning on a different plane. Would it be better to leave well enough alone and not risk losing her altogether? On the other hand, would he ever find contentment in Snowglobe if he didn't try?

He drew in a breath of air tinged with ginger and pine and new puppies. Alone with her, here in the empty store with only the hum of the furnace, the rare wash of lights from a passing car, and the silent snowfall against the windows, anything seemed possible.

"Amy?" he said, and then cleared his throat.

She pulled her hand away, a loss he felt clear to the center of his heart, and pushed to a stand. "I know what you're going to say. We need to get home before the weather worsens. Right?"

His courage, never a problem before, flagged. Heaviness invaded his chest, and he knew his heart was making its own choices.

He stood, too, and shoved his hands in his coat pockets. "Right."

Chapter Eight

The expected blizzard didn't happen, though enough snow had fallen in the night to convince Amy and her mother to bundle up and walk the few blocks to the shop until the snow-plow could do its work.

"Did you and Jeffrey have a nice time in Kalispell?"

"We did." Dana fiddled with her scarf, a bright splash of red against the white snow and black coat. "I hope I didn't disturb you when I got home."

The time *had* been pretty late, much later than Amy's arrival. "I was glad you made it safely in this weather."

"Jeffrey's a good driver. Very experienced. I wasn't worried a bit." Whenever she spoke of Jeffrey, Dana's face lit up, her voice filled with airy optimism. Amy hoped Jeffrey was all he seemed to be. The Caldwell women hadn't had much luck choosing dependable men. "Did everything go okay at the shop?"

"Fine. Well, almost fine."

Her mom shot her a concerned look. "What's wrong?"

"Nothing's *wrong*." She told about the mother dog.

"Oh, honey, you left a dog in the shop all night?"

"What else could I do, Mom? She had babies."

Dana picked up her pace. "She'll destroy the place. Oh, my goodness."

Amy followed along, puffing clouds of fog in the frigid weather, wishing she'd let Rafe take the dogs somewhere. He'd offered but she'd refused, worried about taking the puppies out into the night air.

They reached the shop in record time and Dana quickly unlocked the door, flipped a light and rushed inside.

"They're behind the counter," Amy said. At least, she hoped they were still there.

Before they reached the spot, the mother dog met them, anxious-eyed as she streaked for the door.

"She needs out," Amy said, turning the knob. The dog rushed into the cold.

"I hope she returns for these—oh, look how precious." The irritation in Mom's tone seeped away. "Look at those little darlings."

Four chubby pups of various colors lay in a tangle, sleeping.

"I have no idea what to do with them."

"Call the paper and put in a lost dog ad. Maybe put up some flyers. You can also call Tim Coggins at the police station and ask if anyone has reported a missing dog." Mom crouched beside the pups. Amy suppressed a giggle. Puppies had a way about them.

"What if we put them in the display window with a sign? It's low enough for the mother to climb in and out." Amy asked. "Everyone in town passes here at some point."

Mom glanced up. "My daughter is brilliant. Let's do it. We can fix a basket or box, decorate it up for Christmas, put a bright red bow around the mother's neck. Even if no one claims them, the puppies will attract enough attention to eventually find homes."

She said not a word about the damage a dog and puppies

might do to the gorgeous window display. Mom had a bigger soft spot than her daughter.

In a short time, they'd prepared a tidy bed right in the middle of the lighted Christmas village and transported the pups. When the mother dog reentered the shop, the wiggling, mewling puppies drew her straight to them.

"I've wondered forever what to do with that oversize wicker basket."

"Now we know."

That day they did more business than they'd done the previous three. Everyone stopped to see the puppies and stayed to shop.

"We should reopen tonight after the tree-lighting ceremony," Dana said as she cellophaned a fruit basket. "Business should be great."

"Can't. I promised Rafe I'd help with the sleigh rides." And eat pizza and talk about house plans. Her stomach fluttered at the thought of spending all evening with Rafe.

"What about Mr. Ingerson? He gave the sleigh rides last year."

"He's still bringing his sleigh and horses like always. Rafe's taking the foster care kids for a special ride, carols and hot cocoa at the church."

"That Rafe. He's a jewel."

True. Rafe's hero gene kicked in for the downtrodden. A bitter root boiled in Amy's throat and she fought to swallow it. The whole world was more important to Rafe than she had ever been. He'd proved that when he'd gone into to the military, when he'd gone off to save the world from the bad guys. Now that he was back, his hero gene still ran at top speed.

Why had he invited her along tonight? As a way to apologize or to make her feel better about the past? Somehow that wasn't enough. She'd trusted two men with her whole heart—Dad and Rafe—and both had let her down.

Last night with Rafe and the puppies, a closeness had sprung up between them, and she'd yearned for the past when she'd relied on him without question. The conversation about Mary and Joseph and Rafe's deepening faith had her thinking, too. She wanted to trust that the new, mature Rafe was different.

The cash register pinged as Dana opened it to count the day's till. "You should give him another chance."

Amy's head jerked up. "What?"

"Rafe. He's trying to win you back."

Her pulse bumped. "You think so?"

"Would you be opposed if he were?"

"I don't know. What if it happens again?"

Dana's hand stilled on the register drawer. "Are you willing to spend forever holding yourself away from love because you're scared?"

"No, but…" She shook her head, unsure.

Mom shoved the drawer shut with a *thwack*. "What do you feel for Rafe beyond the fear of getting hurt again?"

Amy picked up bits of paper and ribbon and random trash from the countertop. "Something, definitely something."

"Then start there. Don't rush. You've got all the time in the world. Feel your way along until your faith in him is strong again, until you know whether he's the one or not." Mom pulled her into a hug. "And honey, pray about it. God wants you happy again and so do I. He will lead you."

Amy returned the hug, a soothing balm, as she breathed in the spicy essence of her mother.

Could she do as Mom said? Did she dare put her heart out for Rafe to break one more time? And did God even care one way or the other?

Spurts of childish laughter and excited conversation swirled up into the air along with the powdery snow. A dozen kids of varying ages and types crowded onto Rafe's wagon sleigh.

The two looked gorgeous, and Amy was feeling mellow and full of good cheer as she helped Rafe load a group of foster children into his sleigh. On her way here, she'd run into a former high school classmate, Sara Kincaid, and they'd had a delightful conversation. Amy had been thrilled to reconnect and even happier to see the glow of pleasure when Sara smiled at her date, Owen Larsen. After all she'd been through, Sara and her daughter deserved some happiness. Judging by his tender glances at Sara, Amy had a feeling Owen and his little girl were the ones to give it.

Amy's good mood expanded, warming her from the inside out. Maybe love was in the air this Christmas.

The borrowed draft horses waited patiently, each with a cocked hind foot, while the humans boarded. Amy climbed up, too, her nose cold but her heart warm, while Rafe moved among the children, snugging heavy blankets over laps and legs.

He shot a grin toward Amy. "Ready?"

Thinking about her mom's advice, she returned the smile. "As I'll ever be."

At the irony of her words, she looked away, busying herself with retucking a little blonde girl with freckles.

"Come on up," Rafe called, patting the long wagon seat next to him. "Let's get this show on the road before our jingle bells freeze."

The kids snickered. Amy settled in next to Rafe and with a shake of the reins, they were off. Rafe guided the animals *clip-clopping* through the streets, past the newly lighted Colorado spruce in the center of town where the high school band still serenaded with a concert. Amy turned to face the riders and urged the children to sing along.

An off-key chorus filled the wagon with the lyrics to "Santa Claus is Coming to Town."

Rafe's baritone, full of laughter, joined her soprano. Sides pressed together, she felt the vibrations from his lungs, the warmth of his breath when he angled his face toward her.

They hit a bump and one wagon wheel dipped. The kids' surprised screams quickly turned to giggles except for one child, who started to cry. Amy picked her way to the little boy, who couldn't have been more than six.

Squeezing in next to him, she put an arm around the dark-eyed child. "It's okay, honey. You're safe."

"I'm scared. I want my mama."

Not knowing the boy's situation, she didn't know what to say. Then the older boy sitting behind them leaned up and whispered, "His mom's in jail. He ain't got no dad."

Amy's heart squeezed with compassion. She huddled closer to the boy. "What's your name?"

The boy sniffed. "Robby."

By now, Rafe was looking back. "Problem?"

"Robby got a little scared."

Rafe drew back the reins and stopped the wagon. Rising from the seat, his tall body lean and honed, he came to kneel beside Robby and Amy. "Hey, little buddy. Don't be scared. You ever heard of the marines?"

Amy's stomach curled inward. Marines. Not her favorite topic.

But the little boy stared at Rafe, impressed. "Like army guys?"

"Yes, sir. Close enough. We take care of people." Using his thumbs, he wiped Robby's cheeks. "Especially kids."

The little boy sniffed as he studied the former marine and found reassurance. "Can I sit by you?"

"Sure can." Robby slid off the wooden seat, latched onto Rafe's extended hand and followed him to the front.

Amy's heart turned over at the sight of the man with the boy. Even though Rafe's status as a former marine brought back ugly memories for Amy, it soothed the little boy and she was glad for that.

Gaze trusting, Robby listened to something Rafe said. With an eager nod, the boy climbed in front, between Rafe's knees, and took hold of the reins.

Rafe was letting Robby drive the wagon. The experienced horses could probably drive themselves, but just in case, Rafe kept his hands behind Robby's.

He would make a great dad. But then, she'd thought the same about her own father.

Biting down on her lip, Amy struggled against the negative thoughts. She had to stop this. If they were to ever have another chance, she had to stop throwing up walls of protection. *Sing,* she thought. *Sing!*

"Join me," she yelled to the children, breath a foggy cloud. "Come on, everyone. It's Christmas!"

She chose the liveliest tunes she knew, getting the kids to stomp and clap. When she divided the wagon into twelve groups, assigning each group one of the twelve days of Christmas, they ended in laughter and total confusion.

"Do it again. Again!" the kids shouted.

Amy shot a glance toward Rafe, who looked back with a grin. "I could use some company up here," he said, hitching his chin toward the vacant space at his side. "Me and my buddy need a wind block."

Though her toes tingled with cold, her insides warmed. "Is that supposed to lure me?"

His grin widened. "Whatever it takes to get you up here."

Rafe watched as Amy made her way through the rows of kids, teasing, patting shoulders, giving hugs. She was coming toward him, to be with him. His imagination went crazy for a minute and he saw her with *their* children. In the house he would build, the house that had never been for him. At least, not him alone. It had been for her and he hadn't known it until this moment.

So this was what the Lord had been trying to get through his thick skull. A rich, thrumming assurance filled his chest.

He loved her. Deeper, stronger, better than before, he loved her.

Chapter Nine

The week before Christmas Dana kept The Snowglobe Gift Shoppe open late. Business was brisk, the puppies a popular draw that had garnered an article in the weekly newspaper. To her delight, Sara Kincaid and Owen Larsen had stopped in with their little girls. Janey and Mia were crazy about the puppies, but from all appearances, Owen and Sara had eyes only for each other. Though no one had claimed the dogs, all four fat, healthy puppies were spoken for. The mother, aptly named Ginger because of her brindle color and Christmas arrival, endeared herself to everyone with good manners and a sweet disposition. Amy had a feeling she wouldn't be able to let go of Ginger.

By the time they closed the shop and arrived home, the temperatures had dipped to well below zero and snow fell again. Without a moon, the darkness was absolute.

"We'll have a white Christmas," Dana joked. They *always* had a white Christmas. "What shall we have for dinner?"

The living room lights flickered. Both women looked up and then at each other. "That's not good."

The lights blinked again and Amy headed for the kitchen and flashlights.

"Just in case," she said. Due to the town's older electrical system, they'd suffered an outage last winter. "I hope the power doesn't go down. I want to wrap gifts tonight."

Dana smiled. "Wrap gifts all day long and again at night. The life of a gift shop owner."

"Personal gifts," Amy said with a sneaky grin.

"Personal? How personal? Maybe for a tall, dark and handsome guy who hangs around a lot?"

Amy groaned. "Mom! Stop matchmaking. I'm talking about *your* gifts."

A knock at the door turned them both around. Dana frowned. "Jeffrey's out of town. I wonder—"

Amy opened the door to find Rafe huddled inside his parka, a stocking cap pulled over his ears. His nose and cheeks were red.

Behind her, Dana made little told-you-so noises. Amy could practically hear her thoughts. *See? He hangs around a lot.*

Amy did her best to ignore the noises, but her insides hummed to find Rafe standing in her doorway. Since the sleigh ride, she'd seen him almost daily and it didn't seem to be enough.

He ducked his head and tried to look pitiful. "Do you know where a cold man could get a hot cup of coffee?"

"Oh, silly, get in here." She plucked at his sleeve, pulling him inside the cozy house.

The lights flickered, dimmed and then went out.

"Well." The three of them stood still for two beats, surprised, eyes adjusting to the darkness until Amy remembered the flashlight in her hand and snapped it on. A yellow beam chased away the darkness in their immediate vicinity, casting them in odd, glowing shadows.

"I don't think that could be a breaker, but…" Dana murmured.

"Probably not, but I'll check anyway." Rafe stripped off his coat and gloves. "Where's your breaker box?"

Dana crossed to the window and pulled aside the thermal drapes to look out. "Never mind. The entire block is black. I don't see a light anywhere."

Rafe fished his cell phone from a pocket. "Better call the power company."

Following the quick call, he said, "Power's down all over town. Crews have been notified, but it could be a long, cold night."

"The churches will open for shelter to anyone without a heat source," Dana said. "Otherwise, the best thing to do is stay inside and stay warm the best way we can."

Amy moved to the brick fireplace. "Glad we have plenty of wood."

"You can thank Rafe for that."

Amy's gaze flew to Rafe. She had no idea he'd been their wood supplier this year. "Thanks."

The compliment slid off in a shrug. "No big deal." He rubbed his palms together in a soft shifting sound. "Let's get a fire going."

"Can you stay awhile?" Dana asked. "It's nice to have a man on hand at times like this."

Amy was glad the room was dim, because her mouth fell open. Strong, independent Dana Caldwell was not a delicate, helpless female. The statement was, pure and simple, a ploy to throw Amy and Rafe together. Without making a scene, there was little Amy could do about it—even if she wanted to.

"Be happy to." Rafe joined Amy at the fireplace hearth. "That okay with you, Ames?"

Amy glanced at her mother's shadow. Though Dana's expression was invisible, encouragement pulsed from her.

"Gonna do your famous shadow puppets?"

He grinned. "If I remember how. Got any marshmallows?"

"What kind of establishment would this be without marshmallows?"

He took the log from her hand and positioned it on the grate as they bantered back and forth about silly, meaningless things. She felt good to be natural with Rafe, to just let go and stop worrying about his agenda. Or hers.

"You know what, kids?" Dana's voice interrupted. "I am absolutely exhausted." She faked a yawn, patting at her lips. "I think I'll go to my room, give Jeffrey a call and then call it a night."

"You sure you don't want to roast marshmallows with us?"

"Not that I don't enjoy your company and a good black marshmallow, but this once, I'll pass."

"Jeffrey wins again?" Amy asked and then hoped Mom took the question in the jesting manner it was intended.

Dana leaned down for a hug. She kissed Amy on the cheek. "Love you, darling."

Rafe unwound his long body to stand. Dana hugged him, too. "Night, Dana. Don't worry about anything down here. We got it covered."

"I have no doubt. My daughter and I are in trustworthy hands."

Amy resisted an eye roll.

In minutes after Dana's departure, Rafe dragged the easy chairs in front of the crackling fireplace while Amy scrounged the kitchen by flashlight for marshmallows and candles.

"I'd intended to wrap gifts tonight." She handed him a bag of marshmallows and two skewers.

Rafe ripped open the plastic bag with his teeth. "This is better. We can talk."

"About your house plans?" They were an ongoing discussion both of them enjoyed.

His glance was cryptic. "Among other things."

Her pulse sped up. "What other things?"

A pause ensued while he carefully—perhaps too carefully—threaded a series of marshmallows onto a skewer. "You. Me. Us. Stuff."

"Oh." Tension sprang up inside her, tight like the spring inside an ink pen, ready to fly to pieces if released.

Rafe laid the skewers on the hearth and reached for her hands. "I've debated for days about bringing up the past. Our past."

"I don't want to fight." She tugged her hands loose.

His hopeful expression, gilded by the fire, faded. "I don't, either. I want to explain."

"You explained five years ago. I didn't understand it then and I don't now."

"I'm sorry. Really sorry for hurting you, Amy. I loved you so much and I thought—" He clasped his hands together in a tight fist and glanced away. "I was young and green and gung-ho. A total idiot, I guess, when it came to you."

Amy moved to the fireplace hearth and sat on the hard brick, watching the flickering flames eat away at the wood the same way Rafe's leaving ate away at her trust. "You broke my heart."

"If it's any consolation, I broke my own, too."

She angled to look at him. He leaned forward on the edge of a brown stuffed chair, hands dangling between his knees, his face pensive. Amy wanted to ask why he'd left, why he'd broken their engagement, why he'd thrown away a perfect love. But she knew the answers hadn't changed. He'd believed in a cause greater than himself. Greater than her. The fact that she had not shared his passion had made no difference.

"Talking doesn't change what happened."

"I didn't want to leave you."

"You did."

"I missed you."

She had no response for that.

"Every day, every night, I thought about you. I prayed for you."

His words seared her as if a coal had fallen from the fire into her soul. While she'd been fuming mad and bitter in a safe world, Rafe had prayed for her in a dangerous one.

"Oh, Rafe." She relented and curled her fingers into his.

"I want to put the past behind us, Amy." He tugged at her, pulling her onto the chair with him. "*All* of the past."

She wasn't sure what he meant by *all,* though three tours of war must have left some scars.

She sat next to him, stiff and fearful but yearning for something more than she'd known for the past five years. "I'd like to but…I don't know if I can."

He was silent for a minute while the fire snapped and flared, gilding his rugged face. "Remember the snowglobe you gave me when we were first engaged?"

He hesitated on the word as if afraid of a negative reaction. It still hurt to think about his ring on her finger and those euphoric days. But she was a big girl now.

"I remember. It was a special order."

"Just for me. Engraved on the bottom. I carried that little token all over the world."

"You still have it?" She tilted her face, discovering that her head had somehow become nestled against his shoulder.

"I'll always have it." The short proclamation spoke volumes.

"Why?"

"Because it reminded me of all that was good and right in my life. It reminded me of home and Christmas, and most of all, of you."

A chink of ice broke loose inside of Amy. She imagined Rafe in a faraway and dangerous land watching the swirl of a Montana snowfall, dreaming of home. And her.

In the fire's glow, she touched his cheek with her finger-tips. He turned his face inward and kissed her palm.

Feelings washed over her, warmer than the log heat and every bit as full of light. When he caressed her face with tender tough hands and drew her closer, she didn't resist.

Then his lips touched hers and for a moment she forgot the heartache and long years of mourning. Warm, comforting hands threaded through her hair and held her close. Beneath her touch, Rafe's chest rose, and his heart thudded strong and certain. Emotion swelled in Amy's throat, lovely and longing.

"I never got over you, Amy," he whispered against her lips. "I thought I had, but I haven't."

She'd never gotten over him, either. She yearned to turn back the clock and erase the past and yet, it lingered. Trust once broken was hard to restore. But oh, she wanted to believe. She wanted to believe so badly.

Rafe felt Amy stiffen, felt her withdrawal, her questions and resistance. He ached at her lack of faith in him, but then why should she believe anything he said? Talk was cheap and, in her view, he'd let her down before. When she slid from the chair and changed the subject to easier topics, he didn't push, though he missed her nearness.

He'd not intended to kiss her but he didn't regret it. The remembered sweetness tempered the bitterness of her withdrawal. Something was stirring between, he was certain, and he prayed for a way to earn her trust again.

The evening wore on and still the power remained off. They talked of Christmas and when she admitted to buying him a gift, "just a little something," hope flared again.

They talked of his house plans though the lack of light kept him from whipping out the papers he'd stuffed inside his coat. Yet, when Amy mentioned her preference for white-and-black kitchens, he made a mental note.

They munched on marshmallows and peanut butter sandwiches, debating the virtues of crunchy or plain. When a comfortable silence fell, they watched the fireplace from side-by-side chairs, feet propped on the hearth like an old married couple. He thought about heading home but when he mentioned as much, Amy urged him to stay. The choice was easy. A cozy fire and good company made him linger.

His eyes drooped and he thought of what it would be like if Amy was his wife, if this was their life together. Here, side by side, weathering the storms of life and Montana's harsh winter, dreaming big dreams, comfortable in conversation or in silence.

With a deep, almost contented sigh, he let his head loll against the rough upholstery and closed his eyes.

Amy half dozed in the chair, vaguely aware of the wind whistling at the door and the pleasant heat saturating the bottoms of her sock feet. Another sound intruded and she frowned, resistant to fully waking. Here, in the semidream world, her subconscious could relive Rafe's kiss and the enjoyment of being in his arms again without wrestling with doubts brought on by past hurts.

The sound came again, a groan. Then a mutter. Finally, a sharp cry.

Amy jerked to full consciousness and sat up, alert and listening.

Another groan, this one from Rafe's chair. Amy dropped her feet to the floor and rose, going to him. His head thrashed against the chair, his face bathed in perspiration as he mumbled and groaned against a nightmare.

Amy hesitated, hovering. She'd heard the danger of awakening a soldier recently returned from war.

He cried out, called someone's name, face contorted in misery.

Amy hesitated no more.

"Rafe. You're dreaming. Wake up." She touched his shoulder.

The viselike grip of battle-strengthened fingers closed around her wrist, crushing. She didn't back away, though tears gathered in her eyes. For Rafe, for the pain in her wrist. "Rafe. Please wake up."

His eyelids flew open and he stared wildly, unseeing for one beat and then another.

"Rafe, please, stop. You're hurting me."

Instantly he released his grip. He yanked her against his chest, holding her tightly. His heart thundered, a storm of protest against some inner battle. Face buried in her neck, he groaned, "I'm sorry. I'm so sorry. Are you okay?"

She nodded, throat tight with tears. "Are you?"

"Yeah." But he sounded winded and distraught. "Tell me again."

"You're here, in my house. You had a bad dream."

His face moved back and forth against her hair. "No, you. Are you all right? I'd never hurt you. I didn't mean…"

"I'm okay. You grabbed my wrist, but I'm fine." She held his head, stroked his hair. His body trembled. "You aren't. What happened? A dream about the war?"

He straightened, pushing her away, distancing himself. His lips tightened and when he spoke, he avoided her eyes. "I apologize. That shouldn't have happened. I should go home."

But she knew him too well. Understanding splashed through her. Rafe was embarrassed. For him, a man of iron will and pride, the nightmare was a weakness he could not control.

"This happens a lot?"

He shrugged and stared into the fire. "Some."

She didn't care how much he backed away. He needed her. "You've been to war, Rafe, more than once. You're entitled."

"Marines don't wimp out."

She thought the statement was a bunch of macho nonsense but didn't say as much. "Does your family know about the dreams?"

"Jake knows. We don't talk about it."

Of course they didn't. If they didn't talk about the nightmares, they didn't happen. She mentally rolled her eyes. Men could be such idiots.

"What do you dream about?" Amy realized she was treading on delicate ground, but Rafe had held his trouble inside too long. No matter their painful history, she cared. Her stomach tightened. She would always care. "Only a man with a big, open, passionate heart would be this affected. What you experienced matters, Rafe, and some of it goes deep. There's no shame in caring."

Her words melted him as surely as if he'd been a candle against the fire. His expression eased. His shoulders relaxed, and with a heavy rise and fall of his chest, he said, "I've never thought about it that way. I want to be in control and forget, but when I'm asleep…" He shook his head. "The dreams are nothing specific, a hodgepodge of events and sounds and the general chaos of battle."

Amy slid to the floor in front of him and folded her hands on his knee. In a soft voice, she asked, "What was it like, being in war?"

A log cracked and tumbled, shooting sparks. Around them the house had gone silent, listening, too.

There in the dim, cozy room, safe from war and terrorists, bombs and ambush, he told her. When he finished, a layer of bitterness peeled away from Amy's heart. The fearless marine, the tough outdoorsman, had seen too much, done too much in the name of good and right. War had scarred his soul, and yet he remained the kindest man she knew.

She thought of what else he'd said tonight. He'd kept her snowglobe. He'd shared his house plans. He'd prayed for her.

Amy's heart squeezed.

God was trying to tell her something if she'd stop running long enough to listen. Rafe was a good, good man. A man worthy of love...and trust.

Maybe Christmas was the perfect time for a second chance at love.

Full of hope, she pressed her face against her folded hands, breathed the essence of Rafe's cotton jeans, and prayed. For him, for herself and for the future.

Chapter Ten

The power outage lasted until early the next evening. Rafe had headed to his parents' house long after midnight only to return to Amy's the next morning to be sure all was well. Dana opened The Snowglobe Gift Shoppe without power because of Ginger and her pups, but with the slower business, Amy had chosen, to Rafe's delight, to hang out with him. Business was slow at Westfield Sports Rentals, too, so leaving Jake in charge, they checked on elderly friends and stocked in a new supply of firewood for anyone that needed it.

By the time power was restored, Rafe and Amy had organized an impromptu caroling group for that night.

As they made their way through the residential areas, puffing their joyous song in clouds of vapor, Rafe held Amy's hand. When she shivered, he put his arm around her and was gratified when she snuggled into his coat and smiled up with happy eyes.

Once, when they'd stopped to catch their breath and warm up, he'd stolen a quick kiss. Cold lips collided, and they'd both laughed.

"You need some hot cocoa," he'd said.

"Me? You have lips from the frozen tundra."

"I keep them in the freezer at home. Take them out for special occasions." His eyebrows pumped. "Like now."

His joke brought chuckles from the woman standing next to them. "It's good to see the two of you back together."

With a cocky grin, Rafe hooked an arm around Amy's neck. "Thanks. I couldn't agree more."

Amy's gaze flew to his. When the woman turned to speak with Katie and Todd, she murmured. "We are, aren't we?"

"You good with that? With us?"

Her soft smile seeped into his cold body. "Yes. Yes, I think I am."

Rafe lifted an inner prayer of thanks to heaven. If he'd known telling her about the nightmares would bring her back to him, he'd have told her days ago. She hadn't considered him weak at all. He couldn't quite take that in, but he was relieved she hadn't turned away in disgust.

After a frigid hour of caroling, Rafe invited everyone to his shop where there was room to visit and warm up. On the way, he and Amy stopped at the store for cookies, happy and giddy, toes numb and noses red.

"Grab your favorites. Don't forget the Oreos." He plunked two packages into her arms.

"One for me, one for you. Better get another package for the others to eat."

He chuckled and added a third pack, along with several other brands. "Ready?"

At the checkout counter, they paid, chatting with Stu, the rotund, apron-clad cashier, and a teenage sacker. The talk of the town, of course, was the power outage.

"The mayor stopped by earlier," Stu said. "He thinks we may have to shut down the lights in the park, the town tree and any other nonessentials."

"No way!" Amy said. "We can't do that."

"It's what he said." Stu counted out Rafe's change. "According to the power company, the town system needs an upgrade, which can't be done until spring. If we don't cut back, we could be in for more outages."

Rafe frowned. "Not good for business. Part of the draw for tourists is that Snowglobe looks like something out of a storybook, a picture-perfect Christmas village."

"What about the townspeople? We love our Christmas celebrations, too. They're what sets Snowglobe apart from other small mountain towns trying to stay alive through tourist trade."

"Well, maybe it won't happen." Stu handed Rafe three filled plastic bags.

Of course, it did.

"You're awfully cheery this morning," her mother said.

"Christmas is coming and life is good," Amy said with an airy laugh. She was on her knees next to the low display window, a fat, soft puppy in her arms. The mama dog was outside on her routine run, a perfect time for Amy to clean and restore the dogs' bed.

"I thought you'd be glum about the lights-out proclamation."

"I am. Everyone is. But Jesus didn't have electric light displays and Christmas still came."

"That's true, but I have a feeling there is more to your burst of smiley energy. What's going on with you and Rafe?"

Amy placed the puppy in the clean basket and went to help her mother. "I still love him, Mom."

Dana fisted both hands in contained excitement and then threw her arms around Amy. "I knew it. I always knew it."

"I haven't told him yet, but I think he knows."

"You've always loved him whether *you* knew it or not, and I was sure if you'd give him a chance he'd win your trust again."

A little niggle of fear pushed in, but Amy batted it down. She *could* trust him. He'd done his military duty. He wouldn't leave again. He was home to stay. "He's building a dream house on the outskirts of town, a gorgeous area, and wants my input on *everything*. I think the house is for us."

"Oh, honey." Dana grabbed her hands and danced her around in a circle, laughing.

Customers scattered throughout the store smiled in their direction.

"My daughter's in love," Dana announced to the whole world. Well, maybe not the world, but in Snowglobe, two or three people was all it took to get the word around.

"Mom. Stop it. We have customers." Face warm but smile wide, she went to wait on the women. Fortunately, none of them looked familiar. "My mom is matchmaking. Pay no mind. May I help you with something?"

"We'd like to look at the snowglobes. My husband wants to wrap up our visit today and go somewhere else, and I just can't leave without one of those."

Amy frowned. "I hope you've enjoyed your stay in Snowglobe."

"Oh, we have. We love it here, but without the Christmas lights and festivities…" She shrugged. "Vance wants to go somewhere else."

They were already losing customers and tourists. A shutdown was very bad for business and the town.

When the women left, she said, "Mom, surely there is something that can be done."

"I wish." Dana went back to the flowers she'd been arranging. "But what?"

On his way to Kalispell late that afternoon, Rafe ruminated on the mayor's announcement in the morning paper. All nonessential events and electrical usage, specifically the city tree and festival of lights in the park, would not be turned on again this year.

"The Grinch stole Christmas," Amy had complained when they'd shared lunch at the burger joint. The place had been abuzz with the unfortunate news.

Like everyone else, neither he nor Amy was happy about the turn of events. But no one wanted to be without power and heat, either. The city council's hands were tied.

Businesses would take a financial hit, but at least for today, he and Jake had been renting snowmobiles and skis as if no one had heard about the shut down.

Now, he was in Kalispell to pick up some new equipment his brother had ordered. He also had a personal errand to run.

A pleased grin pulled at his cheeks as he parked in front of Riddle's Jewelry Store and went inside the modern building. He knew what he wanted. He'd spent hours last night researching online.

His thoughts turned to Amy and he replayed the night of the caroling. Since the power outage, she'd changed, softened and their relationship had turned a corner.

When he'd taken her home, he'd kissed her good-night at the door. Then she'd followed him to his truck and kissed him in return.

He'd almost said the words, almost told her of the love he'd carried all over the world, of the love that simply would not die.

He was confident she loved him, too. They were mature adults now ready for a lifetime together. Though they'd not discussed the future, he had faith Amy would agree.

The clerk removed the dainty ring from the display case. "Beautiful choice. A Christmas gift?"

Rafe's pulse increased, a happy adrenaline charge at what he was about to do. "She bought me a little something. I want to return the favor."

The clerk, in slick business suit and tie, smiled knowingly. "This is a lot more than a 'little something.'"

"She's worth it." This, and a lot more. Christmas in Snowglobe was turning out to be the best ever, the electrical situation the only negative. But late last night while he'd laid awake listening to Amy's snowglobe, God had dropped an idea into his head. If he could make it happen…

But that was for later. Amy's Christmas gift was now.

Joy danced inside his chest.

Thank you, Lord, for another chance to do this right.

After paying for his purchase, he pocketed the small black box inside his coat and, grinning like a man in love, turned his truck toward home and Amy.

Four days before Christmas, the day dawned snowy and cold, the streets of Snowglobe dark. Slackened seasonal cheer matched the general downturn in business. The town's mood, however, had little effect on Amy.

Or Rafe, for that matter, she thought, grinning at him over some last-minute Blessing Baskets.

They were inside the family hall at church, empty boxes scattered around their feet. Rafe's iPod played the group Go-Fish and their lively "Christmas with a Capital C."

"I guess we could have called in the other volunteers to help," she told him.

He slid his arms around her from the back and nuzzled the hair at her nape. "And spoil a prime opportunity to be alone?"

She leaned into him, head rested on his strong chest. "So that was your sneaky plan."

"Got a problem with it?" His voice was a low, manly growl.

Amy giggled. "Nope."

In one fast motion, he twirled her around and hugged her close, landing a kiss somewhere in the vicinity of her ear.

"I wonder what Pastor would say about us smooching in the fellowship hall?" she mused.

"Right. Better get busy. We want families to have their baskets in time to make plans."

"I can't believe the way requests keep coming in. All this need is scary."

"Makes you realize how blessed we are, doesn't it?"

They *were* blessed and not just in the financial sense. They were blessed with family and each other. She glanced up into his rugged, honorable face and love swelled like the mountain creeks in spring. "Yes. Yes, it does."

With one last kiss—this one on her nose—he got back to work. Happiness bubbled inside Amy. They were adults now, mature and sensible. Their relationship would work this time.

He pushed a filled basket toward her. "Three to go."

She checked the name and address on the tag. "I'll drive this one out this afternoon while we still have daylight. The roads are passable up that way."

"I'd go with you, but something else came up." He shot her a pleased-with-himself smile.

She tilted her head, curious, and more than a little disappointed that he wasn't riding along on the delivery. "What?"

"An idea to resolve the power problem. At least the part involving the light festival and tree."

"Rafe, that would be awesome! But how?"

"I talked to the Marine Corp Reserves in Billings."

Amy stiffened. "How could they possibly help Snowglobe?" And why would they?

"Since I'm still a reservist, I put in a request to borrow one or two of their tactical generators. Those bad boys can run a field hospital and never sputter. By this time tomorrow, Snowglobe's light displays will be lighting up the whole valley!"

Amy stared at him in disbelief. She'd barely heard the news

about the generators. His good deed came and slipped away again in the wake of the other.

"You're in the *reserves?*" Her voice trembled. Her stomach churned. This wasn't possible.

The shock in her tone turned him serious. "I thought you knew. Is that a problem?"

Amy's lips quivered. She couldn't believe what he was telling her. He was still a marine? "You could be called up."

He shrugged, clearly not understanding the magnitude of his admission. "Not likely, but possible."

She put a wobbly hand to her forehead. Her throat had gone dry as flour. "I can't believe this. You should have told me. I can't do this again, Rafe."

"Come on, Amy. This is not a big deal."

The worry and insecurity exploded in fury. "Not a big deal? You could leave again. You could be called up to fight a war in some far-off place and where would that leave me?"

His eyes frosted over like a winter window, blocking out the light of love. "I would hope that leaves you here, waiting for a man who believes in protecting his country, not behaving like some irrational teenager."

His words whipped through her, a lash that took her breath. "Irrational? You think I'm irrational for not wanting to have my heart broken again? You lied to me, Rafe. You let me believe you were home to stay."

He shoved a hand through his hair. "I never lied about anything. I am home to stay!"

"Can you promise that? Can you promise you won't be called up? Ever?"

His shoulders sagged. "No. I can't." He started toward her, hand out, beseeching. "Come on, Amy. Don't make this a big deal."

She backed away from him, hand up in a stop sign.

"I swore I'd never let you do this to me again, and like an

idiot, I did. But this time, I have sense enough to get out before anything worse happens." She jabbed a finger at him. "Do not come near me. Do not call me. I am done. Do you understand? I'm done!"

She grabbed the Blessing Basket from the table and fled, leaving Rafe with a stunned expression and her name on his lips.

Chapter Eleven

Rafe sank low on the chair inside the office of Westfield Sports Rentals. With a moan, he massaged his aching eyeballs. Marines don't cry, even if their hearts are breaking.

Jake tapped him with a cup of fragrant coffee. "Drink this and tell me what's going on. You look like your dog died."

Gratefully, Rafe sipped at the tongue-searing brew. "Amy."

Coffee gurgled as Jake poured himself a mug and dragged a chair up close to Rafe. "I thought the two of you had patched things up. Last night you were so dewy-eyed I thought I'd be sick."

Jake's joke fell flat.

"I'm not even sure what happened. One minute everything was fine, and then I shared my idea of borrowing a big generator from the Marine Reserves and she went crazy on me." He slurped another sip of coffee. "She said I should have told her, called me dishonest for not telling her I'm a reservist. I thought she knew. I mean, what does it matter?"

"You know, Rafe," Jake said, sounding a lot like their dad. "You've spent a lot of years trying to make peace with that woman and she's done nothing but give you grief." He tapped a hand on Rafe's knee. "Maybe it's time to let her go."

Rafe wagged his head from side to side. "Can't. I love her, Jake."

"I know. That's the lousy part. You always have."

Rafe set the mug aside and rubbed his face with both hands. "What a mess. I don't know what to do."

"Trust me, brother. I'm a man without a permanent woman for a reason. Women will cut you off at the knees and leave you bleeding."

"I never took you for a cynic."

"Realist."

"You've never been in love."

"Never intend to be, either."

The logic didn't make sense, but Rafe was so torn up inside he couldn't think. While he was still wallowing, a customer arrived and Jake went off to wheel and deal. Moments later, the door whooshed open with a purpose and Dana Caldwell sailed inside, red scarf flying.

"We need to talk," she said without preamble. Apparently Amy had already spoken to her mother.

Wrapping his manners around him, he pushed Jake's chair with his foot, a silent invitation she accepted. "I don't think there's anything either of us can say that will make any difference. Amy's done. She broke things off again."

He thought of the ring he'd bought, stored safe and snug in his bedroom. He thought of his dreams, close enough that he could almost see them, but all his dreams and plans included Amy. The ache of loss pushed at the back of his eyelids.

Dana carefully plucked at the fingers of her red gloves to pull them off. "There are things you need to understand."

There were things Amy needed to understand, too. A man had obligations and responsibilities. He started to rise. "*Amy* didn't understand. Not then and not now. We're back where we started and ended five years ago. End of story."

She held up a hand, red fingernails a little too cheery for his mood. "Just hear me out."

Rafe settled back into his chair. He wanted to make things work. He just didn't see how talking would do any good.

"Amy was devastated when her father left us." Dana's chin rose a notch, a proud action that told the humiliation she'd endured at the expense of her unfaithful husband. "When he left, he left us both and never looked back. His abandonment was absolute. We heard from him exactly three times after he told me he was leaving. All three times had to do with the divorce and none to do with the daughter who adored him."

She swallowed hard, a testament to how difficult the loss was for her to talk about, even after years had passed. "I never understood the way he hurt Amy. His beef was with me and what he viewed as my inadequacies as a wife, not with Amy, but when he left me, he left her, too. She never got over him."

Rafe's gut twisted. Dana was a fine woman and beautiful, too. "Any man that doesn't see your value is a jerk."

"Thank you for that, Rafe." Her smile was weak. "You were always a good boy with a kind heart. I know you will never hurt Amy the way her father did, but you need to understand something. She's stuck back there, stuck in his abandonment. When you left, too, she was devastated again. All the pain and rejection came back twofold."

"I never abandoned her! I did what was best for her."

Dana waved off his protest. "That was your perspective. And even though you and I know you had her best interests at heart, Amy didn't believe you. Deep inside, in that place that never healed after her dad left, Amy felt abandoned all over again."

Rafe blew out a long gust of weariness, at a loss. He needed to think and to pray because, in his estimation, the situation looked hopeless. How could he prove to Amy that he'd never leave her again when he might have to do exactly that?

* * *

Amy maneuvered her blue Ford Focus slowly up the snow-packed road and around the mountain toward the home of an elderly widow and her handicapped son. Too proud to ask, the woman and her plight had only come to the notice of the church by accident. Usually, delivering Blessing Baskets filled Amy with joy. Today, all she felt was bereft.

Wheels spun, slipped and then found purchase. Amy refocused on the road, trying to admire the beautiful countryside that so many traveled here to see. Vast pines shot high into a winter blue sky, a sky the color of Rafe's eyes.

She gripped the steering wheel and grumbled. "Even the sky is tormenting me. Why God? Why did You let this happen again?"

She wished she'd never come back to Snowglobe. She'd been fine in Spokane.

Fine, but not in love, a little voice whispered.

"Well, love's not all it's cracked up to be." She flipped the radio on to find a staticky station spewing out cheerful Christmas music. She, who loved Christmas, was annoyed. She snapped the radio off again.

Rafe had accused her of being irrational. Was she? She didn't know. But she was too afraid to take a chance. Mom said she'd never forgiven Rafe, that she was punishing him, when the person she really wanted to punish was Dad.

"Too Freudian," she murmured. She wasn't that messed up.

Snow started to fall in fat, feathery flakes. She turned on her wipers and slowed, gauging the curving road ahead. Several feet of snow lay all around, down the mountain side and into the woods. Regardless of the bitter cold, Montanans lived for this kind of beauty.

She couldn't believe Rafe hadn't said a word about being a reservist. She'd never have gotten involved with him again if she'd known. She'd never have let herself believe and hope and fall in love again.

"Oh, Rafe. I love you. You big jerk. Why can't you just be *my* hero and not hero to the whole world?"

Images of him flickered through her mind. Rafe teaching the little boy to drive the sleigh, packing boxes, laughing back at her as his snowmobile sailed past, the tender look right before he kissed her.

So lost in thought was she that when the back of the car fishtailed, she wasn't ready. Though she grappled at the steering wheel and let off the accelerator, the car seemed to have a mind of its own. Wheels spun, yanking control from her grip. The car careened wildly to one side and came to rest in a tall snowdrift.

For a second, all Amy could hear was the sound of blood pulsing in her temples. She braced her hands at two and ten and pushed back, huffing as if she'd run up the mountain instead of driving. Might-have-beens raced through her mind. She could have gone off the side of the mountain. She could have flipped the car. The distraction of her messed-up life had nearly cost her everything.

Breathing deep to gain her composure, she surveyed the damage. Except for a bump on her forehead and shaky knees, she was unhurt. A few attempts at freeing the car from the deep proved unsuccessful. The jaunty little Ford was stuck.

Dread settled over the initial fear and irritation as she whipped out her cell phone. No bars. No service. She knew that, expected it. Still, losing the connection with help scared her. She was at least six miles from the widow's home and hadn't passed a house in a long time. She was, however, still near a road and Rafe knew where she'd gone.

Her heart sank. Rafe was the only one who knew her exact destination. And they weren't on speaking terms. He wouldn't even know she hadn't returned. She could be out here for days. No rescue was en route. She was on her own.

Lowering her head to the steering wheel, Amy prayed. Then she got out of the car and started walking.

Rafe slammed the hood of an Arctic Cat, satisfied the sleek, powerful machine was serviced and ready for rental. He wiped his hands on a red cloth, grateful for manual labor to keep him busy. The situation with Amy was like a bad tooth, ready to flare up and set him to aching at any given moment.

After stowing the tools in the tall wall chest, he started toward the skis to check which needed waxing. His cell phone chirped.

A look at caller ID and he groaned. Dana. As if he hadn't been gnawing on what she'd told him all afternoon.

"Hello."

"Rafe." She hesitated. "Have you talked to Amy?"

He sighed. "No." The ball was in Amy's court, not his. Talking to her was useless at this point. "Maybe we both need some breathing space."

"She didn't come home."

"What?" His scalp prickled.

"Do you know where she went?"

A glance through the window told him what he already knew. Darkness had fallen. Amy had left in plenty of time to avoid nightfall.

"She's not back?"

"That's what I'm trying to tell you, Rafe. She went to deliver a Blessing Basket and hasn't returned. I can't get her on her cell phone."

"Sit tight. Don't panic." His blood pumped like a jackhammer. "Amy's an outdoorsman and she's smart."

"I'm worried."

So was he. "I'll find her."

Vaguely Rafe heard Dana's sigh of relief as he disconnected, his mind going through the scenarios. What if Amy had had an accident? Mountain roads could be treacherous. What if she was hurt?

The last thought sent him into warp speed.

With a quick explanation to Jake, he geared up, cranked the freshly serviced Cat and roared into the night with only one thought in mind. To find the woman he loved.

He followed the road she would have taken, glad for the choice of conveyance, considering the fresh snowfall. He could move faster and across more terrain on a powerful snowmobile.

In a short time, a bright blue spot against pristine white caught in his headlights. Relief washed through him.

"Amy."

But in seconds he saw what he didn't want to believe. The car was empty. Amy was gone.

Jaw tight, he remounted the machine, mind whirring in prayer and possibility. Tracking in darkness wasn't easy, but he'd done it before. This time nobody was shooting at him. Knowing Amy was out there alone, cold and probably scared, was even worse. With a prayer on his lips and snow quickly obliterating Amy's boot prints, he set off to find her.

Amy's teeth chattered. Her toes had long since grown too numb to feel. She stared around at the dark woods where only the long stretch of snow and wilderness was visible in the moonlight. Where was she?

Bending, she pushed mounds of snow away in search of the road beneath. She didn't find it. Somehow she'd gotten off the beaten path.

She heard a sound, a low growl. Her skin prickled in fear. Grizzly bears lived up here.

"Help me, God." She stared up into the vast, starlit sky, a

glorious sight any other time. "Do You see me down here? I'm lost."

The silly statement made her snort, and she wondered if hypothermia was snatching rational thought. Of course God saw her. He was here, there, everywhere.

She leaned against a tree and considered sitting down for a while to rest. Her legs had grown heavier with each step in the knee-deep snow.

Tired and cold and achy, she thought that a little rest, a quick nap would fix her right up. Back against the rough bark, she slid downward. As her bottom made contact with the powdery snow, she leaned her head back. Rafe flashed behind her eyes. *Get up,* he seemed to say. *You know better. Sleep is deadly.*

She forced herself to a stand, wishing Rafe was here. Wishing they hadn't fought. She wanted do-overs.

"I'm sorry, Rafe." Cold and shaking, she sank back to the powdery earth.

If she froze to death and no one ever found her, Rafe would never know how much she loved him. Tears, the only heat in her body, flooded her eyes.

It came to her then how foolish she'd been to throw away love with a man like Rafe out of insecurity. Rafe loved her. He would always do what was good and right. Wasn't that enough?

He loved her. She loved him. God had given them a second chance. And she had tossed it away like a handful of snow.

She'd been wrong, terribly wrong. Rafe deserved her love and trust, not her juvenile insecurities.

Gritting her teeth, she struggled to her feet once more. She would not allow hypothermia to rob her and Rafe of a future. One painful step at a time, she pushed on through the knee-high powder.

The growl came again and she stopped, heart clattering as she listened hard against the silent white forest.

Grizzly? No. Something else.

Then the growl became a roar and the roar a recognizable sound, a beautiful sound. A snowmobile.

Rafe. I knew you'd come. It has to be you. Please find me.

"Help!" she shouted, but the word was muffled and weak.

In slow motion, as in a bad dream, she tried to run toward the sound. Her legs barely moved, her heavy boots clumsy.

The roar grew louder and she yelled again. "I'm here."

As sure as the snow was cold, Amy was certain the snowmobile rider was Rafe. He was the only one who knew where she was. He was the one who would risk everything to find her. He was the man she could depend on.

A sweep of lights found her but disappeared as quickly as they'd come. She stumbled and sprawled into the burning cold snow, facedown. Hot tears pricked her eyes as she struggled to get up again.

The lights swept over her once more and stopped. A bulky figure charged toward the spot where she knelt in the snow. She lifted her arms and he was there, pulling her tightly against his strength.

"You came. You came. I knew you'd come."

"I'll always find you, Amy."

And then she knew what he'd been trying to tell her along. His love was true and strong and no matter where he was, no matter where she was, he was there for her.

He lifted her from the snow as easily as if she were a child and carried her to the sled.

Shivering, she welcomed the heat packs he shoved inside her jacket and into her hands and boots. All business, he said, "We'll get you warmed up. Drink this."

Amy took the thermos and moaned at the blessed heat of coffee. "I'm okay now. You're here."

"You scared me." The pale, grim line of his lips testified to his statement. "I thought I might lose you, and if I did—" He swallowed, looked to one side.

"I know." If she'd needed proof of his love and commitment, she had it. "I don't want you to lose me. I don't want to lose you. I am so sorry for being an idiot. I love you, Rafe, no matter what."

He swiveled back to her. "No matter what? Even if I get called up again?"

Warmed by the coffee and the truth stirring in her chest, she said, "Whatever you have to do, wherever you have to go, you'll have me here in Snowglobe, waiting. For as long as it takes."

"Thank God," he said.

"Yes, thank God. I prayed. He helped you find me."

Rafe smiled then and pulled her close. "Everything is all right now. You're safe with me."

Amy pressed against her hero's steady, sturdy heart and knew his words were true. Her love was safe. She was safe. Always and forever, she was safe with him.

Epilogue

Springtime in Montana and the purple-pink beauty of the bitterroot flamed against the backdrop of green ponderosas, deep blue mountains and a sky so blue Amy could almost taste it. Saws buzzed and sawdust churned into the sharp, clear air around the site of the home they were building. In the distance at the back of the property, trout leaped and danced for joy in the cold, clear stream running full of icy mountain water.

Amy's feet sank deep in yellow arrowleaf while at her side Ginger quivered with eagerness to run free in the country. All the pups had found loving homes, and their big brindle mother had found hers, too, with Amy and Rafe.

Amy turned her head to watch a mountain bluebird flit and dart in his search for a suitable place to build his nest. The little male bird was a metaphor, she thought, of the basic male instinct to provide a home for his future family.

She stuck her hands inside the pouch of her sweatshirt. Rafe was doing the same for her and for the children they'd someday have.

The thought made her smile, and filled her with a joy she could not express in words.

That terrible day when she'd gotten lost had changed everything. She knew now that not only was Rafe a man to love and trust, he was a man of action. He would always be a giver, a hero to those in need. True to his word, he'd delivered generators to restore the town's light displays, and Christmas in Snowglobe had gone off without another hitch. And if his country called, he'd serve with strength and commitment and the promise that she would be proudly waiting for his return.

Beside her, Rafe rolled up the house plans and put his arm around her waist. "It's coming along."

"I love it." She leaned into him. "And I love you."

"Does this mean you're ready to set the date?"

Amy held out her left hand. The beautiful diamond he'd given her on Christmas sparkled in the sunlight. "I've been ready. You were the one who wanted to wait for the house to be finished."

Do things right this time, he'd said, and she'd agreed. They'd build first, and after the wedding, they could start life together in their dream home.

"The builder says he'll be done before the snow flies again." He turned to her, smiling and confident. "Want to marry me today?"

"Actually, yes. Today. Right now. We can live in the back of my shop."

He shook his head and laughed. "Don't tempt me. Waiting is hard even when I know it's for the best."

And that was the way Rafe was and one of the many things she loved about him. He would always do what he thought was best. He always had. Now she understood how very important that was. This was a man who would always have her best interest at heart.

"One wedding at a time," she said. "Let's get Mom and Jeffrey married first." For indeed, they'd set the date for midsummer and Amy had come to love the gentle man who loved her mother.

"He's a good guy. They'll do great."

"I know. I'm so happy for Mom." The Snowglobe Gift Shoppe was hers now and thriving, as was Rafe's rental business. They would build a good life here, a life that would carry into future generations of sturdy, winter-loving Montanans.

Her joy surged, a great wave that reached out and pulled in everything and everyone around her. God had answered her prayers. He'd sent Rafe when she'd needed him most, and He had taken away her fear. Somehow, through Rafe's act of Christmas courage, she'd let go of her anger and unforgivingness and embraced the love and goodness that had been waiting for her all along.

"A Christmas wedding would be nice," she said, touching his beloved face with her fingertips. "Christmas brought us back together."

"The only thing better than Christmas in Snowglobe is a Christmas wedding in Snowglobe. Especially if it's *our* wedding." He took her cheeks between his hands and kissed her with all the love in his big hero's heart.

"It's the busiest time of year."

"Doesn't matter." He gestured at the house. "Another Yuletide homecoming sounds perfect. This one as man and wife."

"Yes." She smiled, gazing into his rugged face. "We'll be coming home again, and this time, it's forever."

Ginger leaped up to chase a butterfly. Birds twittered in the towering pines. Amy and Rafe joined hands and started across the yard where someday their children would laugh and play. Together, as man and wife, they'd face the future, knowing as they leaned on their faith and on each other, life would be as beautiful as a Christmas in Snowglobe.

* * * * *

Dear Reader,

I had such fun creating the town of Snowglobe, along with fellow author Lissa Manley. I hope you enjoyed the journey to the beautiful mountains of Montana and felt the warmth and love of *A Snowglobe Christmas*.

Since Christmas is my favorite time of year and nothing says "Merry Christmas" like a good recipe, I thought I'd share one from my family to yours. It's easy-as-pie and just as delicious.

PEPPER JELLY CHEESE SPREAD

1 8-oz block of cream cheese
1 jar of mild pepper jelly—or hot if you prefer
1 box of your favorite snack crackers—mine is Ritz

Place the cream cheese on a pretty plate. Pour ½ cup of pepper jelly over the top. Line the sides with crackers. And you have a pretty, tasty snack in a hurry.

Until next time,
Merry Christmas,

Linda Goodnight

Questions for Discussion

1. Can you describe the story's setting? Did it add to the tone of the story? How?

2. Who were the main characters? Could you relate to any of them? Who was your favorite and why?

3. Pinpoint the romantic conflict. Each character felt justified in his/her response to the situations. Which character do you agree with? Why?

4. Rafe is ashamed of his nightmares. He believes they are a sign of weakness. Do you agree? Why or why not?

5. At one point, Amy experiences a sense of loss when she learns her mother has a boyfriend. Do you think this is a typical reaction, even for an adult? Does a divorced woman have a scriptural right to date and if so, under what circumstances?

6. The town of Snowglobe experienced a power outage. Has that ever happened to you? Describe your reactions. Was the town council right to shut off all the light displays?

7. What is the climax of this story? Describe the moment when Amy changes. What changes her and why?

A FAMILY'S
CHRISTMAS WISH

Lissa Manley

To Pamé, for your sympathetic ear,
wonderful friendship, unwavering support
and much-appreciated cheerleading. Love ya!

Trust in the Lord with all your heart, and do not rely on your own insight. In all your ways acknowledge Him, and He will make straight your path.
—*Proverbs* 3:5–6

Chapter One

As Owen Larsen walked up the snow-covered front path of The Snowglobe Bed-and-Breakfast, he flipped his three-year-old daughter Jane's hood up onto her head. Fat snowflakes silently drifted to earth, blanketing the ground in a glittering coat of white.

Of course, they'd be having a white Christmas; it had been snowing solid for almost a day, which was pretty much the norm in Snowglobe, Montana, this time of year.

"Daddy, I like snow," Jane exclaimed in her cute, high-pitched voice, holding her hand up to catch a few flakes. "Pretty."

He hiked her further up into his arms, pressed a kiss to her forehead, then carefully headed up the rock stairway that would take him to the front door of the B and B. On his way, he noted that the stairs had obviously been shoveled earlier but were getting covered again, quick. "I know you like it, sweetie." Anything white and fluffy captivated Jane.

This would probably be the last regular snowfall he and Janey would see in quite a while; from what he understood, Moonlight Cove, Washington, their soon-to-be home, was known more for precipitation of the liquid variety than snow.

No matter. He was after a fresh start and an escape from

heartbreaking memories, not good weather. And after praying to God for guidance, Owen firmly believed the job waiting for him in Moonlight Cove, Washington, was what he needed since Kristy had died a year ago. Hanging around this town wasn't high on his list now that Kristy was gone.

Shifting Jane again, he raised his hand to knock on the door, which was flanked by 1930s style narrow leaded glass windows depicting snowy mountain scenes. Very appropriate landscape for a Montana mountain town that was covered in snow for a good part of the winter.

Jane squirmed in his arms. "Want down, Daddy."

He obliged and set her on her feet, hoping Sara Kincaid, the owner of the inn and the person he was coming to see about repairing her roof, didn't mind that he'd brought Jane along for their estimate appointment.

Sara had sounded pretty desperate on the phone this morning, and given that his babysitter, Mona, had to go out of town due to a family emergency, he'd had no choice but to bring Janey along. He'd need to find a temporary sitter while he cleaned up some loose job ends before they left town in two weeks.

"Take my hand," he said to Janey. She grabbed it just as the door opened, and then, all three-year-old shyness, sidled over and hid behind his leg.

Sara Kincaid stood on the other side of the doorway, and his breath hitched just a bit as he got a look at her this close. He'd seen her in town since she'd moved here a few years ago, of course—Snowglobe wasn't that big—but always from a distance. He'd had no idea how all-out pretty she was with her wavy, long dark hair, gorgeous hazel eyes, and creamy complexion. She wore dark jeans and a long-sleeved forest-green shirt that complemented her green-tinted brown eyes really nicely.

"Mr. Larsen. Thanks for coming out on such short notice." Her eyes snagged on Janey, and Sara smiled gently. "Oh…and who do we have here?" she asked, raising her brows, keeping her voice soft and kid-friendly.

Owen looked down, pressing a hand to the back of Jane's head. "This is my daughter, Jane. My babysitter had to go out of town suddenly, so I had to bring her with me."

Sara squatted down. "Well, hi there, Jane."

Janey buried her face in the back of his leg, remaining silent.

"She's a bit shy," he said. "Once she warms up, though, she's not shy at all."

"Lots of kids are that way," Sara said, looking up at him. The winter light hit her eyes just right, turning them to the color of gold-flecked pine trees.

The sound of running feet echoed through the air, and a blonde, curly-haired dynamo of small girl who looked to be about Janey's age blasted into the foyer and literally skidded to a stop next to Sara. The girl wore pink leggings and a pink-and-purple-striped shirt with a pink horse printed on the front.

"Hi!" She smiled, then caught sight of Janey peeking out from behind his legs. The girl tugged on Sara's sleeve. "Mama, why her here?"

"Although, as you can see, this one isn't shy," Sara said with a quirk of her brow. She put her hand on top of her daughter's head. "Mia, this is Jane. She's here with her daddy, who's going to help me with the roof. Remember I told you he was coming?"

The girl pursed her lips. "I *bemember*." Her mouth broke into an impish grin as she regarded Jane, her head canted to the side. "I'm Mia. I have a kitchen in my room," she said, only she pronounced it *woom*. "Wanna see it?"

Janey's hand loosened on his leg and she moved a few inches away from him, eyeing Mia, clearly interested in the girl's offer. A play kitchen was a big draw, and there was nothing like another kid—and an outgoing one, at that—to get a shy one to relax.

"Well, either way," Sara said, moving back. "Let's all get inside where it's warm."

In tandem, he and Janey stepped into the house, which he noticed smelled like cookies baking. His mouth watered; Kristy had always been the baker in the family, so he couldn't remember the last time he'd smelled the scent of homemade cookies.

Just as he started to unbutton his fleece coat, Mia reached out and took Janey's hand. "Let's go. I let you use the *oben*."

Janey looked up at him.

Sara closed the door and piped in, "Her room is right around the corner."

"Go ahead, honey," he said, applying gentle pressure to Janey's narrow shoulder. She hadn't started preschool yet—no sense in starting here when they were on the verge of moving—so it would be good for her to socialize with a child her own age.

After a moment's hesitation, Janey followed Mia down the hall and around the corner, shedding her coat as she went. They were almost exactly the same size, one blonde and one brunette. Cute.

He looked at Sara, then went over and picked Janey's coat up off the floor where she'd unceremoniously dropped it. "I hope you don't mind that I brought her. As I said, my babysitter had to go out of town to tend to her ill sister, and I haven't had time to find alternate care."

"No problem. Mia loves to play with other little girls." She held out a hand. "Can I take your jackets?"

"How old is she?" he asked, shrugging out of his coat. "They look about the same age."

Sara took the jackets from him and draped them over on the antique oak hall tree just below the stairs. "She turned three last month."

"Janey'll be three next month," he replied.

"Ah. Two peas in a pod, then."

"Looks like it." He gazed around the small foyer, taking in the large garland-festooned oak staircase rising directly in front of them as well as the parquet flooring and raised oak paneling so popular in 1920s and 1930s style architecture. "This place is gorgeous. Was it built in the thirties?"

She tilted her head to the side. "I'm impressed. You're close—it was built in 1929. How did you know?"

"I'm an architecture buff, and I've done some woodworking in my day." Although, not since Kristy had died. Being a single dad didn't allow him time for hobbies. Or much of anything, really. Not to mention he just hadn't had the heart for much socializing since he'd lost Kristy.

He wondered if he ever would.

"How long have you been running this place?" He'd heard somewhere in town that Sara, a Snowglobe native, had moved back and taken over the B and B. He'd also heard that she was a single mom, but he didn't know the details of that story. Looked like they were in the same boat, though, as single parents.

A shadow crossed her eyes. "I inherited it from my great-aunt, so when…um, life threw me a curve, I came back and converted it into a bed-and-breakfast."

Curve? Yeah, he was familiar with those. "How's business?" he asked, noting the distinctive absence of guests. In fact, except for the sounds of the girls drifting in from around the corner, it was dead quiet. The parlor to the left of the foyer was empty, despite the fire crackling in the fireplace and glittering Christmas tree just visible in the far corner.

Another glimmer of distress flashed in her eyes. "Not so good. With the roof leaking, I've had to cancel a weeklong booking of people in town for the ski race."

Of course. Lots of people came to town for the annual event. "Oh, wow. Seems like this kind of stuff crops up at the worst times, doesn't it?" He only hoped whatever was wrong with her roof could be taken care of quickly, before he left town.

"No kidding," she said. "Winter should be my busiest time, and I need to have good occupancy to keep this place going, so I really want to get the roof fixed as soon as possible."

"Let's go take a look," he said, gesturing up the stairs for her to proceed him. "I take it the problem is upstairs?"

She started up the staircase. "Yes. This place has three bedrooms up and one down, which Mia and I share. So she and I have a place to sleep, but because the party booked needed all three guest rooms and I only have two available right now because of the leaking, they canceled."

"Couldn't you book a smaller party?"

"I suppose I could have, but I didn't want to given I was going have a contractor banging on the roof for the next little while."

He saw her predicament. "Ah, makes sense." He hesitated on a stair. "You think the girls will be okay?" he asked.

"We'll only be up here for a few minutes."

"Okay, lead the way."

She showed him the wood-paneled bedroom affected by the water damage, and his attention was immediately drawn to the beautiful, period antique furnishings and carefully coordinated wallpaper and accessories. He also took note of how she'd paid attention to the finest details in the room, down to the wicker baskets filled with water and packaged treats suitable for a late night snack.

He was really impressed. Obviously, Sara had put a lot of work and expense into this place.

When he got a look at the damage, though, his heart sank a bit; she had some pretty serious water leakage going in the bedroom she'd shown him, which he suspected had been brought on by the recent heavy snowfall.

Once he'd seen what he needed to see, they went downstairs and checked on the girls who were happily "cooking" in Mia's kitchen. And then, with Sara's promise to watch the girls, he went outside, grabbed his ladder off his truck and climbed up on the roof to take a closer look.

Sure enough, the snow had put weight on some worn areas of the shake roof, which had then caused leakage when water had hit some rusted flashing. All in all, a bad situation. And not one that could be fixed quickly.

Unfortunately, he wouldn't have time for this job.

Sara was waiting for him in the foyer when he came back in the house. "So, what's the verdict?" she asked, her voiced tinged with worry.

No sense in sugarcoating things. "You've got a pretty bad situation up there."

Her brow furrowed. "Oh, no."

He briefly explained what was going on. "You're going to need new flashing, repair and a lot of new shakes."

"How much is that going to cost?"

"Ballpark, probably at least a thousand dollars."

Her eyes widened. "That much?"

"To do the job right with good quality materials, and keep future leaking under control, yes."

She pressed a hand to her mouth.

"Sorry. Obviously, I don't like delivering bad news. But I don't think I should minimize the situation. That tactic won't do you any good in the long run and might ultimately end up costing you more."

"I appreciate your honesty." She sighed, pressing a hand to her forehead. "It's just that…I hadn't planned on this expense."

"It's not something you should wait on, either," he added. "With the snow falling and piling up, it'll only get worse, especially when it warms up and all of that snow melts."

She nodded. "I have to be honest with you, Mr. Larsen."

"Call me Owen."

"Okay, Owen." She shoved her hands in the front pockets of her jeans. "I don't have the money for these repairs."

He blinked, not quite sure how to respond to that. After all, he was a businessman, with his own expenses to cover—if he had time to do the work, which he didn't.

She held up her hands. "Before you respond, I have a proposition," she said, lifting her chin.

"Go on." No harm in hearing her out, and he just didn't have the heart at the moment to zing her with the bottom line.

"You said you needed day care for Jane while your babysitter is out of town."

"Yes," he said, suddenly seeing where this was going.

"So, do you think we could work out some kind of exchange, day care for roofing work?"

He rubbed his jaw, regretting her idea wasn't going to work. He'd really like to help her out, and her offer would be an ingenious solution to both of their problems. "Normally, I'd say yes."

"Normally?"

Nodding, he went on. "But Janey and I are planning on leaving town in a few weeks, and I don't have time for this job."

"Leaving town, as in *permanently?*" she asked.

"Yep. I've had a job offer in Washington State, and I want to get there before Christmas."

"Oh, dear," she said, chewing on her lip for a few moments. "I don't mean to be rude, but may I ask why you even came over if you didn't have time for the work?"

Valid question. "I was hoping the job could be done in a few days, squeezed between my other jobs, before we head out. But to be done right, that's not the case, and I don't want to cut corners to fit a tight timeline."

"Okay, I can appreciate that." She spun around, her head down.

Owen felt about as big as a gnat.

She turned back around, her expression set, yet deliberately so. Obviously she was putting on a brave face. "Well, thank you for coming by." She grabbed his coat and handed it to him.

"Would you like me to call someone else for you? Art Cramer is good and reliable, and he won't try to rip you off."

"Unfortunately, unless I can exchange day care with Art, I can't afford to pay him."

"Art's kids are all grown," he replied, regretting that wasn't an option for her.

Her eyes clouded over. "Oh."

Owen paused, torn. He wasn't the type to leave someone high and dry; in fact, if he weren't leaving town, he'd take her up on her deal in a second and give her a big discount, too. He knew all too well how rough it was being a single parent.

Besides, he'd been raised a Christian and had been taught to help others whenever possible; his mom was always helping someone out in the small Seattle suburb in which she and Dad resided, usually with him by her side.

"But that's not your problem," Sara said, her jaw set at a stubborn angle. Clearly she didn't ask for favors often.

He liked that. Probably more than he should.

Before he could respond, Mia and Janey came running out, each dressed in princess costumes and carrying plates of pretend food they'd "cooked" in the play oven.

"Look at me, Daddy!" Janey crowed. "I a princess that can cook!" She spun around, her face glowing.

Mia giggled. "Me, too!" She twirled around. "Look at us!"

In unison, they laughed, then ran off together, presumably for more cooking and dress-up.

His heart lifted. He couldn't remember the last time Janey had had so much fun. Sure, she was generally a happy kid; he was there for her as often as possible and made sure she had everything she needed. But the fact remained, she could use a new friend to play with.

And the new friend's mother needed someone who could repair her roof.

That would be him.

He looked at the ceiling. How could he refuse? He could reschedule the Wilson family's job for next week, sure. They were out of town for the holidays, anyway, so that job was flexible. And he could call Art and ask him if he could take on Ben Montrose's deck repair. He was guessing that would be no problem, seeing as how Art was semiretired and free to do odd jobs that came along.

Owen's brain clicked forward, and he suddenly remembered that his old foreman Jeff Rogers owed him a favor. Maybe he could help Owen out, and they could get the job done in record time if they worked long hours. Plus, he had to have day care for Janey in order to finish up his other jobs. He needed this arrangement.

He turned to Sara and said, "If I can get help, I'll reschedule another job, hand one off to Art and do the work for you. Even Steven trade for day care."

"Oh, no, that trade isn't even. I'll pay you something," she insisted. "Maybe for materials?"

He held up a hand. "We'll settle up those details later." Pulling his cell phone out of his pocket, he continued on. "Let me try and rustle up some help."

Some of the worry lines smoothed out, and she tipped him a small smile. "Oh, thank you, thank you so much. You're really helping me out of a bind."

With his eyes lingering on her brilliant smile just a little too long, he nodded an answer. Then, to distract himself, he found Art's number in his cell's directory and pressed the dial button.

And hoped he didn't regret tomorrow his decision to come to Sara Kincaid's rescue today.

Chapter Two

As the sound of pounding on the roof echoed overhead, Sara pulled the chicken pot pies she'd made for dinner from the oven.

She was truly grateful Owen had decided to fit her repair in and that Jeff had been able to assist. Though she preferred to do things on her own, she knew when to let the experts take over. And the truth was, she'd had no choice but to rely on Owen's and Jeff's roofing expertise to fix her problem.

Setting the fragrant main course on the counter, she put the potholders down and headed to the room she shared with Mia to check on the girls.

Sara peeped around the doorjamb, smiling when she saw Mia and Jane having a tea party on the bed with several of Mia's stuffed animals. They were still dressed in their princess costumes. At this rate, they'd wear out Sleeping Beauty and Cinderella and Sara would have to get the sewing machine out and make some fresh girly dress-up costumes.

Her heart squeezed with satisfaction. Janey was an absolutely darling girl, and having a playmate for Mia was a real blessing. Things had turned out very nicely since Owen had come by yesterday to give Sara an estimate. He'd handed off a job to Art and returned that very day to start repairing her roof with Jeff. They'd worked until dark then, and were well into another long day of work.

Satisfied everything was well with the girls, she went back in the kitchen and grabbed the plates and utensils to set the table in the dining room. She set four places, hoping Owen took her up on the offer she intended to make to have him stay for dinner. It was the least she could do for him given that he was insisting they make their deal an even trade, despite the fact that his roofing work was worth much more monetarily than a few days of day care.

He'd refused anything less, and desperation had forced her to agree. She was still thinking about ways to pay him at least something for his work. If he were staying in Snow-globe, she'd offer free day care for as long as he needed it. Since that wasn't possible, she'd come up with something else for sure. Even three meals a day wasn't going to compensate him adequately.

As she tossed the salad, she sent up thanks to the Lord for sending Owen to her just when she needed him the most. Despite the hard times Josh had brought on by walking out on her when she'd been almost nine months pregnant, Sara still believed God would provide, and that had been proven when He'd provided a kind, caring, skilled contractor like Owen.

Good-looking was on the list, too, but she wasn't thinking about that.

The pounding from overhead stopped abruptly, and Sara cast her gaze out the kitchen window. Dark was falling fast, which undoubtedly had forced Owen and Jeff to stop work.

Time to round up the girls for dinner. Owen would have a hard time refusing if they were all sitting around the table, ready to eat, when he came in to get Jane, and Sara was determined to present him with a hot meal after a long day of work.

And Jeff, too, for that matter, she thought, then hurriedly set another place at the table. They were working hard in cold, snowy weather, and would probably be starving. A warm meal would do them both good.

Besides, Owen was a single dad—everyone in town had been shocked and saddened when his wife had died of cancer a year or so ago—and would probably welcome a home-cooked meal he didn't have to make himself after a grueling day's work.

Though Sara hadn't personally known Kristy Larsen, given that Sara had generally kept to herself since she'd moved back to Snowglobe, by all accounts Kristy had been a lovely person, loving wife and wonderful mother. Sara's heart broke for Owen and Janey; losing someone you loved was always hard, as Sara well knew. But having to stand by and watch your spouse die? She couldn't even imagine. Her heart broke for the Larsen family.

Five minutes later, she had the girls sitting in booster seats at the dining room table, their sippy cups in hand. The meal she'd prepared was spread out on the large, round antique dining table Sara had refinished, a literal smorgasbord of yumminess. What could she say? She loved having someone to cook for, especially someone who would undoubtedly appreciate good comfort food.

She heard the front door open and then close.

"In the dining room," she called out.

A few seconds later, Owen appeared in the arched opening separating the parlor and dining room. His dark eyebrows rose as he took in the cozy dinner scene before him.

"Daddy!" Jane waved. "You eat dinner *wif* us?"

He moved into the room and took off his knit hat, exposing his short, slightly wavy dark hair. How he didn't have a terrible case of hat-hair was beyond Sara. His dark blue eyes roamed over the spread on the table, which included the pot pies, homemade dinner rolls and Waldorf salad, one of Sara's favorites, mainly because her mom had made it often when Sara was growing up.

"Uh…I don't know," he said, blinking, clearly taken off guard by the ready-and-waiting meal.

"You can ask Jeff to stay, too," Sara said. "There's enough for everyone."

"Jeff had to get home for some kind of family dinner," Owen said, his eyes snagging on the pot pies sitting front and center. "Is that pot pie?"

"Yes, it is. My aunt's recipe."

"It smells delicious," he said. "And I am hungry…"

"Oh, trust me." Sara grinned, nodding. "It's out of this world."

"Please, Daddy. We stay." Jane held up her sippy cup. "I have milk!"

Owen regarded Sara. "You sure it isn't an imposition? Because I have a gourmet frozen macaroni and cheese waiting to go into the oven when I get home, and, hey, that's hard to pass up."

"I'm sure," she replied, liking his sense of humor.

He paused, then said, "All right." Shucking off his coat, he set it over the back of his chair and cast his gaze around. "Is it okay if I go wash up?"

"Of course."

"Be right back."

On his way, he dropped a kiss on Jane's head and waved at Mia. Sara did her best not to notice how good he looked in his jeans and long-sleeved waffle weave T-shirt…but the guy was in some shape from swinging a hammer and carrying building materials around all day long. And he was a really nice guy. A nice *single* guy…

Horrified, she veered away from that thought as if it were an angry porcupine. Her dad and Josh walking out on her was enough to last a lifetime. Or two. She'd never willingly set herself up to be dependent on anyone ever again. For anything.

And even if she were willing, Owen was leaving town

soon. Why ask for trouble? He would fix her roof. She'd take care of Jane for a few days. They'd maintain a friendly relationship, and then they'd both go on their merry way, no worse for the wear. Easy.

Determined to keep her thoughts of Owen in check, she started filling the girls' plates, giving them each a small portion of everything, hoping they'd eat a bit of all of it.

Just as she set each plate in front of Mia and Jane, Owen returned. His hair was damp around his face; he'd obviously really freshened up. "Wow. You outdid yourself," he said, sitting and spreading his napkin on his lap. "This is quite the meal."

A glow of pride spread through her. "I like to cook, and I'm used to making food for a group." She held out a hand for his plate.

He handed it to her. "Ah. Of course, hence the 'breakfast' in Snowglobe Bed-and-Breakfast."

"Correct." She filled his plate with generous portions of each dish and two rolls and gave it back to him. "I also include dinner in my rates and often pack picnic lunches for my guests."

"Do you also do all the housework and upkeep around here?" he asked as he buttered his roll.

"Sure do."

"And you take care of a three-year-old all day?" He picked up his fork. "That's a lot of work for one person."

"Yes, it is." Sometimes it was overwhelming to be on her own, with so much responsibility. But she'd take that reality any day over letting someone else be in control of her future. She'd done that with Josh, only to have him leave her high and dry when he'd decided late in her unplanned pregnancy that he didn't want to be tied down to a child. It was a heartbreaking pattern established when her dad had done the same thing to her mom when Sara was ten. "But it allows me to be with Mia and to be my own boss."

"Still, it's gotta be hard to keep this place going by yourself." He took a bite of pot pie and nodded, clearly appreciating the dish.

"It is, and sometimes I need help and I call people like you." She served herself a more modest portion of pot pie, salad and a roll. "Unfortunately, with a house this old, I have to do that more often than I'd like. Just last month, I had to have a plumber come and fix some leaky pipes, which is why I'm short on funds to take care of the roof." She pursed her lips. "Speaking of which, I'd really like to talk about some kind of payment plan."

"We already figured that out," he said.

"No, you generously offered to trade some work for daycare, which, believe me, I appreciate." She leaned over and cut Jane's pot pie into smaller pieces. "But it's obvious that deal isn't really equitable, and I'd like to find some way to pay you in full eventually."

He chewed for a moment, then set his fork down and wiped his mouth with his napkin. "Look, I've been working all day, and I'd rather not talk business. Can we just table this discussion for now and enjoy this great meal with our daughters?"

"Yes, of course we can," she said, realizing he was right. "As long as we don't put it off permanently."

He paused, peering intently at her. "You're not going to let this drop, are you?" he asked, smiling crookedly.

"No, I'm not." She took a sip of water. "I don't like being beholden to people." As long as she relied only upon herself, she'd be fine, and her heart would stay intact.

"Beholden?" He frowned, then leaned back in his chair. "Is that the way you view this situation?"

She pushed her pot pie around her plate. "Well, yes." Guess that's what happened when the one person you trusted most in the world kicked you in the teeth and then left you there, bleeding. She was extra vigilant now against making the same mistake.

"Really?"

"Is that weird?" she asked, wondering if she was coming across as a bit off her rocker.

"Not weird, exactly, but maybe a bit…leery?"

"Maybe." She tapped a finger on the table. "Let's just say I have my reasons for wanting to shoulder my fair share."

"Such as?" he asked.

"Oh…various things," she said, raising her brow and glancing at Mia and Jane with a slight tilt of her head. Sometimes adults had to have in-depth conversations when little ears weren't open wide. And, of course, she was sure Owen wouldn't be interested in her tale of woe. He had a more heart-wrenching story for sure; hers would seem petty in comparison.

He paused briefly, then nodded, obviously understanding. "Oh. Okay. Gotcha."

They finished the meal—Owen had seconds of everything—and then they cleaned up the girls and cleared the table. He insisted on helping with the dishes, and no amount of shooing would get him to change his mind, so Sara relented. He washed and she dried, and they worked there side by side in the glow of the muted kitchen lighting, with the steam from the hot water in the sink rising around them, all warm and comforting.

The girls played happily at the small table in the kitchen, barking as they pretended two stuffed dogs were real, and best puppy friends to boot.

It occurred to her then that she couldn't remember when she'd enjoyed an evening more, and that perhaps she might be a bit lonely for social company; she was a busy single mom running a business, and she had virtually no time to herself. That thought of liking spending time with Owen had uneasiness blossoming inside of her, and she sagged back on the counter for just a moment.

Then she drew herself up, chiding herself for overthinking

the situation. This work trade arrangement was just temporary. As long as she didn't get used to having Owen around—and she wouldn't let herself, she vowed—she'd be fine.

When the dishes were done and put away, Owen took out the trash and Sara finished wiping off the counters. She lit a kitchen candle to freshen up the room after an afternoon of cooking, and when Owen came back in, everything was clean and put away, ready for the next meal.

"We'd better go," he said, looking at his watch. "It's getting late."

She looked at the clock on the wall. Only seven o'clock. "For a three-year-old," she said, quirking a rueful smile.

"Right," he said, returning her smile.

She found her gaze lingering on that appealing lift of his lips. "Although, these days, I'm pretty tired myself by this time of night."

"Me, too. Parenting is exhausting, isn't it?" he asked. "Especially for single parents like you and me."

She nodded. Those softly uttered words hung in the air, somehow signifying a silent yet unmistakable kinship that burned like a banked fire in Sara's chest. He understood the challenges of her life, she thought. Better than a lot of people....

They gathered up Jane's things, and despite the girls' pleas that they wanted to play tea party "just one more time," everyone headed to the front door.

Sara handed him Jane's pink parka. "She'll need this tonight. It's cold out there."

He took it from her. "No kidding." He bundled Jane up and flipped the fur-trimmed hood onto her head, then looked out the stained-glass windows by the door. "I think it's snowing again."

"It's supposed to snow all night," Sara replied. She'd need to shovel the stairs and walkway again in the morning.

"Snow!" Jane exclaimed. "Pretty!"

Mia giggled and jumped in the air. "Pretty snow!"

"Maybe I'll take them out to play in it tomorrow," Sara said. "We can make snow angels."

The girls cheered and danced around the foyer, flapping their arms like angels.

"Speaking of tomorrow," he said, grinning at the jubilant three-year-olds, "I'd like to get an early start again since daylight is so limited this time of year. Okay if I'm here as soon as it's light, around eight?" He bent down to put Jane's boots on.

"No problem," Sara said. "We're early risers." Mia rarely slept past six.

"Great."

An idea occurred to her. "In fact, why don't you guys come for breakfast? I have a new cinnamon roll recipe I want to try, and it makes a ton."

He straightened. "I don't want to put you out."

"You won't be. Really. Actually, you'll be helping me."

He blinked and stared at her.

"I need taste testers," she said.

He cleared his throat, then crouched and put on Jane's other boot. "Who am I to deny you use of a taste tester?"

"Great. Then I'll see you in the morning."

"Right," he replied, zipping up his coat. "I'll look forward to those cinnamon rolls."

As he and Jane walked outside and down the stairs, Sara noticed that someone had shoveled all of the snow off them, and the walkway, too.

"Owen," she called, holding up a hand.

He turned around as he put on his hat.

"Did you shovel the stairs and the walkway?"

"Yup."

How had she not heard him? Maybe he'd done it when she was vacuuming? Her heart glowed warm. "Well…thank you," she said. One less thing for her to do tomorrow. Good, right?

"You're welcome."

With Mia by her side, Sara stood on the wide front porch and watched Owen and Jane make their way to his truck parked at the curb, their boots squeaking in the snow. Fat flakes continued to silently drift down, floating to earth in the glow of the porch light.

Owen loaded Jane into a car seat in the cab of his truck, then with a wave, went around the vehicle and got in. The ignition started and they drove away, the red taillights of the truck glowing like Christmas lights in the dark street until they disappeared from view.

Her breath forming fog in the wintry air around her, Sara stood for a moment, her hand pressed to her chest, still taken aback by his thoughtfulness; having someone else looking out for her was a foreign occurrence for sure.

Foreign, yet somehow comforting, knowing her load had been lessened by some small yet still significant amount. She had someone else to rely on, even if just for a little while.

As she hustled Mia into the house and closed the door against the cold, Sara cut off those warm and fuzzy thoughts with a quick yet effective mental slap. She depended on nobody but herself. With that reality echoing in her head, she sternly told herself to appreciate Owen's gesture, but not to get used to having him do things for her, or to count on him for much. He would remain nothing more than her roofing contractor and temporary taste tester. No matter what, she had to remember that to protect herself. And her heart.

Chapter Three

Owen shook the snow from his hat-covered head and stomped his feet on the stoop, then stepped into the warm foyer of the bed-and-breakfast.

Satisfaction settled down around him; he and Jeff had made good progress on Sara's roofing job over the course of the past week. Now it was Saturday, and though he typically didn't work on weekends so he could spend time with Janey, he was glad he'd done so today. If they kept up at the rate they were working, they'd be done in plenty of time for him to finish up the Wilson job before he and Jane took off for Moonlight Cove. Art had willingly taken over Bill Montrose's deck project and had welcomed the work. He'd said his newly retired wife was driving him crazy at home.

Funny how Owen couldn't quite understand that sentiment. In his world, husbands and wives enjoyed each others' company. Wasn't his place to judge, though, and who knew? Maybe the work arrangement might actually be good for Art's marriage in some twisted kind of way.

The scent of roasting meat hit Owen as soon as he closed the door. His stomach grumbled and he had to admit, he was enjoying Sara's cooking. A lot, since she was quite good in the kitchen. And she was really kind and generous, both to him, and more important, to Jane. And…well, no question she was easy on the eyes.

That thought was confirmed when she stepped out of the kitchen, her finger pressed to her lips in the universal sign for "be quiet." She wore a festive red-and-green apron over a cream-colored turtleneck, slim jeans and black, fur-trimmed boots. Her hair was piled up in a loose bun and tendrils of glossy chestnut hair waved around her rosy face. No question, she possessed a fresh-faced beauty he really found appealing.

"What's going on?" he whispered, surprised at how glad he was to see her. Shocked, actually; he'd never had even an iota of interest in any woman but Kristy since they'd met in college, and certainly no one since she'd died. What was going on indeed—a loaded question to himself if he'd ever heard one. Loaded, like an automatic nail gun in the wrong hands. One twitchy finger or bad aim, and someone went down.

Sara moved closer, pointing to the parlor. "The girls fell asleep on the couch, and I'd like to let them sleep a few more minutes until dinner is ready," she whispered.

He stepped forward and craned his neck. Jane and Mia laid end to end on the couch, both conked out while Big Bird spouted lessons on the TV in the corner. "Ah, okay," he replied, smiling at the sight of the snoozing twosome. "What did you do? Make them run a marathon?"

"Nope," Sara said, an impish grin on her face. "We just played in the snow all afternoon."

"I saw. It looked like you guys were having a great time."

"Did you see the snow girls we built?"

"Nice touch, the cookie eyes, carrot noses and pink scarves." He'd watched Sara help Mia and Jane build the snow girls from the roof as he'd been working, and he'd been impressed by her patience and creativity, not to mention her kindness toward Jane. Sara clearly loved children, and he knew his daughter was very fortunate to be able to spend even a little time with her. For that reason alone he was glad Sara and Mia had come into Jane's life, no matter how briefly.

"Thanks." She motioned him to follow her into the kitchen. "They insisted on dressing them in something pink."

"It's Janey's favorite color," he said.

"Mia's, too."

His mouth watered even more as the scent of what smelled like pot roast and roasting potatoes filled the air. "Do I smell pot roast?"

"Yep." Sara grabbed two oven mitts from the counter and opened the oven. With a flourish she pulled out a huge roast. "My aunt Tasha's recipe."

"Smells great," he said.

She put the roasting pan down on the stove and patted the oven. "This baby has made this dish hundreds of times, and I thought tonight would be a great night for an extra hearty, rib-sticking meal."

"Why's that?" he asked.

"The town tree lighting is tonight, and Mia and I will be out later than usual." She looked at her watch. "Oh, where has the time gone? We'd better wake the girls up so we can eat. The lighting starts promptly at seven."

Owen's stomach clenched. "I didn't realize that was tonight." Or more like he hadn't *wanted* to realize the annual tradition was tonight. He and Kristy used to go to the lighting every year, and somehow the thought of attending without her just hadn't seemed right since her death.

"It's always the third Saturday in December." Sara turned to him. "Are you guys going?"

"No."

"Oh." She raised her brows. "Why not? Pretty much everybody in town goes, and I think Jane would love it."

He paused, wondering what to say to that; she was right. Even so, he wasn't quite comfortable with hanging his memories of Kristy out on his sleeve.

"I'm sorry for prying," Sara said as his silence stretched out. "I'm sure you have your reasons."

"I do." Lots of them.

"But if you want to go, Mia would be thrilled, I'm sure, to have her new best friend with her for the event."

He stalled, torn. "I don't know…" On the one hand, the prospect of facing the ceremony without Kristy filled him with a hollow numbness he'd rather cut off in its tracks. But on the other hand, Janey would love the experience. She'd already commented on some of the Christmas lights on houses around town and had asked about Santa Claus a couple of times lately. Besides, he knew the event was designed for all ages, and the town went all out with the whole Christmas theme. There would be carolers, cookie decorating, popcorn stringing and gingerbread-house-making booths and, of course, Santa would be putting in an appearance.

No doubt about it; tonight, the Snowglobe Town Square would be the place to be for just about everyone in town, kids most especially. Could he really deprive Janey of that Christmas cheer, all because he didn't want to face memories of Christmases past? Trouble was, he couldn't.

He looked at Sara standing patiently by, waiting for an answer. "All right, we'll go." He was all about what was best for Janey.

Sara clapped. "Great. Mia will be thrilled!" Sara headed toward the parlor, talking over her shoulder. "Let's get the girls up, have us some rib-sticking pot roast and potatoes and then bundle up and head down to the ceremony."

He followed Sara into the parlor, wondering about the wisdom of his decision given how many memories were sure to surface during the event. It might be an emotional night for him, and the last thing he wanted was to get upset in public.

He nudged Janey awake as Sara did the same to Mia. Both girls woke up slowly, rubbing their eyes as they sat up.

"Time to get up, sleepyheads," Sara said. "We have to eat so we can go to the tree-lighting ceremony in town."

Janey blinked up at him. "We go, too, Daddy?" she said hopefully, gazing up at him with those big blue eyes of hers.

Toast. He was toast. "Yep, we are, honey."

"Yippee!" she and Mia said in unison. They both jumped off the couch, their sleepiness gone, and bounced around the room, crowing in high-pitched voices about Christmas lights, Santa and the cookies they'd be decorating.

Sara looked at him, then nodded toward the girls. "Guess we made them happy."

Exactly. "Guess we did." And in that moment, he knew without a doubt that experiencing the wonder of Christmas through his daughter's eyes was worth any price.

"Mama, look at my cookie!" Mia said, her eyes sparkling.

Sara bent down and admired the Christmas-tree-shaped cookie Mia had decorated with white frosting and green and red sprinkles. "Nice job," she said, wiping a bit of frosting from Mia's cheek.

They'd arrived in town and made a beeline for the cookie-decorating station at Porter's Bakery so the girls could do that before the tree-lighting ceremony. At the moment, Mia and Jane were alone at the table, although Sara was sure a fresh wave of kids would show up any moment.

Janey had her head bent down as she meticulously covered her snowman cookie with different colored dots of frosting. Red, green, yellow. Red, green, yellow.

Sara looked at Owen, who stood behind his daughter. "She's quite the little artist."

"Yeah." His mouth curved into a sad smile. "She got that from Kristy, who was the artistic one. Unlike me." He shrugged. "I still draw stick figures."

"I'm not a very good artist, either," Sara said. "I should

do more artsy projects with Mia, but I have no idea how to go about it."

"Kristy was very creative and was really excited to be able to share her love of art and crafting with Janey." He shook his head. "She actually wanted to start teaching children's art classes when Janey got a bit older and had already picked out supplies and furniture for the space in the third bedroom of our house. She had a whole plan in place."

"Kristy sounds like she was a wonderful person," Sara said softly.

"She was," Owen replied so quietly she almost didn't hear him. "She was an amazing woman."

Sara's heart twisted; clearly, he was still struggling with Kristy's death. Who wouldn't be? He'd suffered a terrible loss—the loss of love.

Sara understood that, at least.

Though her instincts told her to offer support, now wasn't the time. Instead, she simply nodded to acknowledge his statement, and then bent to take the sprinkles away from Mia. "Hey, there, sweet pea. I think we have enough sprinkles." She turned a rueful gaze up to Owen. "Can you say 'sugar high'?"

"Oh, yeah." He pointed to Janey's cookie, which was now heaped with multicolored frosting dots.

It was time to go and let some other kids decorate. Sara cleaned Mia up with the baby wipes provided while Owen did the same for Janey. And then they stepped outside, handed the girls their cookies and let them nibble as they headed to the tree-lighting ceremony across the town square.

The roads around the square had been closed, so there was no traffic to deal with, not that there was ever that much in Snowglobe. Still, it was nice to be able to walk in the street and not worry about watching for cars.

Thankfully, it had stopped snowing a few hours ago, and the skies had cleared. So rather than having blizzard cond tions for the event, it was simply a very cold, clear night, with the moon slung low in the dark night sky, the stars twinkling in the background.

As she took in the picture-perfect scene before her, Sara snuggled into the scarf around her neck, glad she had dressed warmly. It was going to be a chilly night for sure.

Snowglobe had come alive for this night—the town council had strung tiny white lights on all the trees lining the town square and had put big red bows on the streetlights. The huge Christmas tree in the center rose up, a dark mass just waiting to be lit with thousands of multicolored lights it had taken volunteers days to string. Carolers strolled around in groups, singing joyous Christmas songs, their breath forming misty clouds in the freezing night air.

Nothing said Christmas like this festive night in Snowglobe.

She slanted a glance at Owen as they walked, noting his strong profile beneath his hat. What was it about him that drew her attention so? Sure, he was handsome. But there was something else there, something that had her thinking about him at the oddest times.

It had been obvious back at her house that he'd been reluctant to come here tonight; she guessed that he and Kristy had probably attended the ceremony together at some point—everybody in town turned out for the event, which was doubling as a fund-raiser for the local hospital this year—and that maybe he was worried about sad memories surfacing. But he'd agreed to come, for Janey's sake, Sara was sure, and she really admired him for putting his daughter first, even when it was clearly difficult for him.

He was a good dad, and examples of that had been few and far between in her life.

Maybe that was the reason she was so drawn to him, because she liked the kind of parent he was. And because he was so unlike her own father and Mia's dad. In a very good way, of course.

Whatever the case, as long as she kept her feelings firmly entrenched in the "like" category, she'd be fine. Anything less than complete emotional vigilance would be dangerous; Owen was leaving in a few weeks, end of story.

Feeling on a more even kilter, Sara stopped next to the bookstore, noting that both Mia and Janey had frosting all over their hands and faces again. "Get a load of them," she said, motioning to the girls. "Did they eat cookies or just frosting?"

"I come prepared," Owen said, producing a few more wipes from his coat pocket. "We're gonna need these."

They cleaned the girls up once more and were soon on their way to the center of the town square.

Sara said hello to several townspeople she recognized as they ambled along, including Amy Caldwell, a friend from high school, who'd moved back to town to run The Snowglobe Gift Shoppe, which her mom, Dana Caldwell, owned. Rumor had it that Amy was seeing her ex-fiancé, Rafe Westfield, just back from a few tours in the Middle East with the marines. They'd been together since high school but had broken it off when Rafe had left to join the military. Sara knew Rafe had crushed Amy's heart by leaving; another reminder to Sara to keep her own heart safe.

Though Sara hadn't socialized hardly at all since she'd moved back here two and a half years ago, she had grown up in Snowglobe, and knew lots of people who'd lived in these parts for ages. She had to admit, it was nice to come out from under her rock for a while and actually interact with the community.

To Sara's delight, the girls oohed and ahhed over the glittering lights displayed in the shops' windows. Just about the time they stopped to admire some pretty decorations in the window of the florist, Sara heard sleigh bells echoing through the square.

"Oh, look!" she said, pointing left. "Mr. Ingerson is running his horse-drawn sleigh!" Sara knew Mr. Ingerson in passing, and had ridden his sleigh a few times over the years at the tree lighting.

A few moments later, the sleigh, pulled by two huge palomino Percheron draft horses with long, silky flaxen-colored manes, glided around the corner a half a block down.

"Look, Daddy!" Janey exclaimed. "Horseys!"

Mia jumped up and down. "I love horseys!"

As luck would have it, the sleigh headed toward the curb just in front of Sara and Owen and the girls, and then with a gentle "whoa" from Mr. Ingerson, pulled to a smooth stop right there. The horses obediently stood, their huge necks arched, foggy breath puffing out of their velvety noses.

"Pretty horseys," Mia said. "I love them!"

The horses were decorated with green-and-red ribbons in their manes and tails, and the sleigh was covered in twinkling white lights. The leather straps that went over the horses' shoulders were adorned with bells that jingled merrily as the animals moved.

Mr. Ingerson tipped the stiff brim of his bright red hat. "Hey, girls. Would you like to be my first ride of the evening? There's plenty of room for all four of you." His gray mustache twitched and his eyes twinkled. "If you don't mind getting a bit cozy."

Sara looked at Owen as she tried to ignore the thought of getting "cozy" with him. This wasn't that kind of evening. "What do you think? Do you want to go?"

"I do!" Mia said.

"Me, too!" Janey added.

Owen canted his head to the side and quirked his mouth. "Who am I to say no to a group of adorable females?"

"Excellent!" Mr. Ingerson wrapped the thick leather reins

over a hook on the side of the sleigh and then alighted. "Allow me," he said, holding his hand out for Sara. "You and your gentleman friend will need to sit and hold the girls on your laps."

With Mia and Janey squealing in delight, Sara climbed in first, followed by Owen, who then leaned over and lifted each girl into the back of the sleigh with Mr. Ingerson's help. After Owen put Mia on Sara's lap, he sat down, barely fitting in the leftover space next to Sara.

She suppressed a gasp at the feel of his broad, solid shoulder pressing against her own. He was a big guy and the seat was very small for two adults with three-year-olds on their laps.

Mr. Ingerson got back in and settled in the front seat. As he took up the reins, he turned, those eyes glinting again. "You'll have to put your arm around her," he said to Owen, nodding toward Sara. "It's a better fit that way, and warmer, too." He winked.

Oh, Sara doubted she could get any warmer.

"He's probably right," Owen said, shifting to the side. A pause. "Um...do you mind?"

Sara cleared her throat. "Not at all," she replied, her voice high-pitched, even to her own ears. "It'll probably be more comfortable." In some ways. But other ways? Not so much.

"I agree." Owen leaned to the side and lifted his arm, then hesitantly placed it stiffly over her shoulder, almost as if he were afraid to touch her.

Sara's heart pounded at the contact, and she deliberately held herself awkwardly upright, needing to keep some kind of barrier, no matter how small, between them for her own sanity.

"So, girls," Mr. Ingerson said. "Are you ready for Caramel and Latte to take us on a ride?"

As he spoke, the horses stomped their feet at the sound

of their names, obviously raring to go, and the sleigh bells jingled a cheerful tune.

"Yes!" Mia and Janey squealed, each bouncing up and down on the lap they sat in. "Let's go!"

With a cluck, Mr. Ingerson set the horses into a smooth walk.

Sara's breathing was anything but smooth. It had been a long time since she had been this close to a man, and just the feel of Owen's heavy arm over her shoulder set her pulse skittering.

A block into their ride, he squeezed her shoulder where his hand rested. "We both should just relax," he said, regarding her with a slight smile. "It's only a sleigh ride in tight quarters."

"Oh. Right. Yeah." She forced herself to loosen up enough to lean against his side.

"It'll be more fun for Mia and Janey that way."

Good point. She consciously relaxed, letting herself snuggle into his side, reminding herself as she did that this sleigh ride, this closeness, this whole evening, actually, was for the girls' benefit. Not for her and Owen to get to know each other better. As long as she remembered that necessary reality, she'd be fine.

But she had a feeling that with Owen's arm around her and his spicy scent drifting to her, despite the chill night air, remembering what was important was going to be pretty much impossible.

Chapter Four

After a moment's heavy anticipation, all of the lights in the town square went out. Collectively, the crowd gasped right along with Owen. And then, instantly, the giant tree in the center of town lit up, a brilliant display of twinkling multi-colored lights that cast their glow over the awestruck crowd fanning out from the base of the tree in all directions.

"Oh, Daddy!" Janey said from her spot in his arms, her voice filled with wonder. "It's bee-yoo-tiff-ul."

He squeezed her tight, then looked down at her face and saw the magic of the season produce a radiant smile. "Yes, it is, isn't it?"

He'd expected to be sad when he saw the tree light up without Kristy by his side. He'd counted on the upsetting emotion, actually. So much so he hadn't even considered coming to the lighting ceremony last year. Surprisingly, though, while there would always be a part of him that missed Kristy and grieved for her, seeing Janey so cheerful, so filled with Christmas wonder, made him realize that coming here tonight with Sara and Mia had been the best choice he'd made in a long time.

His daughter was happy, so he was happy. A simple concept he needed to remember.

And he had Sara to thank for that profound realization.

As that thought crossed his mind, he turned and rested his gaze on her. She wore a cream-colored knit hat, and her dark hair fell in waves to below her shoulders. A matching scarf graced her neck, and he'd noticed when they'd been in the bakery watching the girls decorate their cookies that the color of the scarf and hat made the most of her creamy complexion and hazel eyes. The lights from the tree lit up her face in a very flattering way, and he thought again how pretty she was.

As he surreptitiously watched her, she held Mia close, then pressed a tender kiss to her chubby cheek before turning her own sparkling gaze up to the tree. Owen's heart jolted a little; her love for her daughter was as plain as day on her face.

Seeing Sara's maternal devotion to Mia reminded him that Janey would miss a mother's love for sure. For the rest of her life. As usual, that knowledge bothered him, partly because it wasn't his choice for Janey, obviously. And also partly because he wasn't an idiot; his need to keep such strict control of his love life was in direct conflict with what would probably be best for his little girl both now and in the future.

As he watched Sara with Mia, he let his mind go to a forbidden place. Should he rethink his desire to remain alone? Funny how he'd been considering the same thing when they'd taken their cozy sleigh ride earlier. With Sara pressed close to his side, not only had he enjoyed her nearness—a lot—he'd also enjoyed being part of a family again, or what resembled one on some level.

He'd realized as the girls' giggles had echoed in the chilly night air, mixing with the sound of the sleigh bells, that he missed the companionship and connection and happiness a romantic relationship brought into his life. He wasn't stupid; he understood in the deeply practical part of his male psyche that though he loved Janey with everything in him, loving a woman could provide something important that being a dad never would.

Was he willing to take the risk to have that in his life again?

Before he could come up with an answer, Sara looked over and caught him staring at her, and her clear gaze held his. He didn't even try to look away; he was enjoying the view way too much, although he knew he liked much more about Sara than her looks. She had a good heart, a gentle way and a loving demeanor that was hard to ignore. But he would, he vowed.

After a beat of time, her glossy lips curved up into a shy, almost private smile, and right then and there his heart almost quit beating.

Sara looked away first, flushing a bit. "Janey, honey, look up top at the tippy top of the tree!" she said, laying a gloved hand on Janey's shoulder.

He managed to pull his gaze from Sara, and then looked up at the same time Janey did. There, at the very top of the tree, was a brilliant star made out of hundreds of twinkling golden lights.

"A star!" Janey exclaimed.

"A pretty star," Mia echoed.

"Every year," Sara explained in an expressive voice that held his and the girls' attention, "Jim Sanders makes a new star for the tree in his metal shop. I can remember when I was a kid how excited I was every year to see what the star would look like."

"I like this one," Mia said. "And so does Janey, so it's the best one."

"You think? I don't know. There've been some awfully pretty ones in years past." She regarded Owen with a slanted brow and speculative gaze. "What do you think, Owen?"

Looking right at her, the truth came blurting out. "I think the one in front of me is the prettiest one I've ever seen."

She blinked, but recovered quickly. "Um…you're not even looking at the star," she said in a mock scolding tone.

"I know," he replied, laying an arm around her shoulder and pulling her and Mia so close he could smell the shampoo Sara used. Something fruity. And wonderful.

With an audible sigh of what sounded like contentment, Sara wrapped her free arm around his waist and snuggled next to him, fitting perfectly. The pom-pom on her hat tickled his nose and her warmth seeped into him, heating him up from the inside out.

Mia and Janey chattered excitedly about the tree, the cookies they'd decorated and, of course, Caramel and Latte, the prettiest horses in the whole wide world. A group of carolers strolled by, singing something about it being the most wonderful time of the year. With rapt wonder, Mia and Janey held hands and listened to the song, their faces shining bright with Christmas joy.

His heart turned over at the sight, and a sense of peace settled around him. And try as he might to shove his happiness aside to keep himself on the safe, practical road he'd always wanted to trudge, he simply couldn't manage to steer himself clear right now. With his daughter's happiness so obvious and his own contentedness impossible to ignore, he admitted to himself on the spot that the words to the song the carolers sang were true.

And for the moment, that unmistakable truth was all he would allow himself to think about, even though he wasn't foolish enough to think he could ignore harsh reality for very long and still protect his heart.

"I had a really great time tonight," Owen said to Sara as he gently put a drowsy Janey into her car seat in the cab of his truck parked in front of Sara's house. "Thank you for asking us to go with you."

Sara watched as he carefully lifted the harness over Jane's head and clipped her in, then leaned over and picked up three stuffed animals and handed them to her one by one before he stroked her rosy cheek. He grabbed a few more and tucked them in next to her so she was literally surrounded by softness. "All cozy and comfortable, honey?" he asked Janey, leaning in.

She nodded, laid her head back and put her thumb in her mouth. Sara guessed she'd be asleep in seconds. It had been a big night for everybody.

Sara shifted a sleeping Mia in her arms just as Mia snuggled closer and then laid her head on her shoulder.

"I had fun, too, and so did the girls," Sara said. "I think the sleigh ride was the highlight for them. I've already had to promise to take them to see Caramel and Latte at Mr. Ingerson's farm."

Owen grinned, shaking his head. The glow from the clear Christmas lights he'd quickly strung on the porch railing as a surprise earlier today cast his handsome face in a warm, rosy glow. "What is it about little girls and horses, anyway?" He grabbed a stuffed horse from the seat next to Janey and held it as backup to his statement.

"Want horsey," Janey murmured sleepily, holding her hands out.

He handed the fluffy brown horse with a long mane to her. "I'm guessing this will be her favorite animal for quite a while," he said, opening the driver's door to turn the heat up full blast in the truck. It would be warm and toasty in there quickly.

"You're probably right," Sara replied. "I'm pretty sure there will be a lot of horse-themed stuff added to Mia's Christmas list this year."

He closed the truck's door, then shoved his hands into his coat pockets. "Maybe we'll need to go shopping together."

An undeniable thrill shot through her at the thought of spending more time with Owen, but she quelled it pronto. "Okay."

"I could really use some help with buying girly stuff for Janey."

"I'm your gal, then," Sara said, hefting Mia up in her arms. How could one three-year-old get so heavy? The wind kicked up, chilling the tip of Sara's nose. She should probably go in, but somehow she felt compelled to stay and talk with Owen. Maybe because adult conversation, without a couple of three-year-olds interrupting every five words, was a rare occurrence for her.

"Here. Let me hold her for a while," he said, reaching out.

Without hesitation Sara gently gave Mia to him, not completely oblivious to the significance of her willingness to hand her daughter over so readily.

Slightly breathless, she took a long look at Owen, adoring how he held Mia in his strong arms, all fatherly and profoundly protective.

Precisely the kind of love and affection neither Sara's nor Mia's father had ever shown her. Mia's father hadn't even loved his daughter enough to stick around for her birth, much less for her whole life. What a flake. Amazing how hindsight worked.

Sara felt her defenses toward Owen trembling and her vulnerability meter ratcheted up, rattling her even more.

She shook her head. *Get a grip, girl.* He was talking a shopping trip between friends, not a date. She could handle that. But more? No way, no matter how much a tiny part of her wanted so much more than a toy shopping trip with the wonderful man cradling Mia as if she were the most precious thing on earth.

Well, it was official: he'd lost his mind.

Owen drove slowly home from Sara's house, his gloved hands tight on the steering wheel. Janey slept in the seat behind him, conked out, and the Christmas lights on the houses on this section of Main Street cast weird shadows on the interior of his truck.

What had he been thinking, suggesting he and Sara spend more time together, even if it was only toy shopping?

As in…a date?

He yanked his hat off. He didn't date. Not since Kristy. Didn't want to. He felt as if he were setting himself up for a world of hurt if he cared about someone other than his daughter.

Guess that's what happened when cancer, the ultimate control thief, did its thing and robbed you of one of the most important things in your life.

He navigated his way on the deserted, snow-covered streets toward home. Sure, Christmas lights and decorations glowed bright and cheery in almost every front yard. It was the merriest time of the year. So what was with the aching hollowness that had been throbbing in his chest off and on ever since he'd met Sara?

That question echoed in his head as he hung a left on Glacier Lane, then took a quick right onto his street, Icicle Drive. His house, a small, neat ranch built in the fifties, came up quickly on the right, and he carefully turned into his driveway.

He sat there in the dark as the truck's heater blasted hot air, looking up at his shadowed, unadorned house, thinking it looked sad and lonely surrounded by his neighbors' houses glowing bright.

He suddenly wished he'd put Christmas lights up this year, even though he and Janey would be leaving before Christmas day; maybe he should embrace the holiday season, even if just for a short time. Janey would love it, and that alone made decorating the house seem worthwhile. He hadn't packed the Christmas decorations yet. Maybe he'd haul them out tomorrow.

He inched forward into the garage, put the truck in Park,

then got out to get Janey. With a sleepy murmur she settled into his arms as he took her out of her car seat, and she threw her arms around his neck.

Love for his little girl unwound inside of him, true and deep and unwavering. He had Janey and would forever. And that would be enough.

Holding on to that thought, he headed inside, punching the garage door button before he went in. He paused in the family room. The place was cold and dark and silent, and a nagging sense of aloneness seeped through him. There was no Christmas tree glowing in the corner, no decorations brightening up the place. In fact, the house was filled with half-packed boxes and piles of stuff waiting to be packed. Not exactly homey.

And there was no one waiting here for him, no one sitting by the fireplace with a smile on her pretty face, a mug of hot tea in her hands and a warm touch just for him. On some level, he was well and truly alone, and if he kept on the path he'd laid out, he always would be. His chest hitched.

As he moved through the family room and went down the hall to Janey's room to put her to bed, a vision of Sara rose in his mind and the tightness in his chest eased a bit, warmth spreading through him like a healing tide. She always had a way of raising his spirits, of making him feel like he had hope in his life.

With that thought swirling he tucked Janey in, gave her a kiss good-night and then went to the kitchen to get a drink of water before bed. He stood there, alone in the dark, knowing he had a cold bed waiting for him down the hall and not much else. Like a dead-center hammer strike, the reality of his life hit him full force.

When he wasn't a dad, he was by himself. Since Kristy had died, he'd been single by choice, and that had been enough in the past. But he'd met Sara and spent time with her and her daughter, and by contrast, his life alone seemed black-and-white and drab.

A prayer rose from his lips, and he hoped God would show him the right path in the coming days. And would help him determine if what he'd chosen for himself would ever be enough in the future now that Sara had lit up his life with her beautiful smile, caring ways and the uncanny ability to break his walls down with nothing but a touch.

Chapter Five

Sara raised her voice in song as the sweeping sound of the church organ filled the sanctuary. Her spirits took flight; she loved singing her praise to the Lord in concert with the other parishioners of New Life Church.

Undeniably, church hymns always had the power to fill her with a sense of joy and warmth, even in her darkest hours when Josh had left and she'd been alone, nine months pregnant and about to become a single mom. She would always have her faith, no matter what.

Thank you God, for sticking with me. Your comfort and guidance means the world to me, and I know I can always count on You.

She sneaked a glance sideways, happy that Owen and Janey were seated in the pew next to her and Mia. She'd invited them to attend church at the tree lighting last night. Thankfully, Owen had readily agreed to attend the service as a group; neither one of them were very good at saying no to their darling daughters. Sara had told herself that this his-and-her church experience was strictly for Mia and Janey, who would go off to their Sunday school class in a few minutes. Although, Sara had to admit, having an adult friend to worship with was wonderful for her, too. What was it about sitting next to someone at church that was so comforting? Perhaps mutual faith tied a strong spiritual bond. Which might speak of other possible bonds…?

Veering away from that idea like it was a hot potato—why get caught up in something that wouldn't last more than one or two services?—she trained her eyes on the hymnal. She put a lot of effort into concentrating on singing well, since Owen possessed a fine baritone that put her own iffy soprano voice to shame.

The hymn ended on a swell of praiseful sound, and then Pastor Jacobsen stepped up to the pulpit.

"Parents," he announced, "the Sunday school teachers will now come row by row to get the children for class."

Owen leaned over. "Here's where it gets dicey," he said close to Sara's ear.

She gave him a questioning look and tried to ignore how her heart sped up when he was close, how good his spicy aftershave smelled. How nice he looked in his sport coat, tie and pressed black slacks. And especially how much she liked him sitting by her side, his leg almost touching hers. Nothing but trouble there, but the thought plagued her nonetheless. "Dicey?" she managed.

"I've never been able to get Janey to go to Sunday school. She always cries and gloms onto me like a vise."

Sara swung her gaze to Janey, who was already standing alongside Mia, holding her hand, her face shining with bright-eyed eagerness while they waited for Teacher Heather to collect them. "Um…she doesn't look worried now."

"Let's hope for the best," he replied with a doubting lift of his brow.

Teacher Heather, a fresh-faced, slender woman in her mid-twenties who had a three-year-old son in Mia and Janey's class, arrived at their row.

"Are you ready, Mia?" Teacher Heather said with a welcoming smile, holding out her hand. Her eyes alighted on Janey. "I see you have a friend with you today."

Mia nodded as she moved by Sara and Owen, Janey in tow, without so much as a goodbye to Sara. "Uh-huh. We're going to play with the dollies before we learn about Jesus."

"I already know 'bout Jesus," Janey said on her way by. No goodbye or tears or clinging from her, either. In fact, she didn't even look at Owen. "I just want to see the dollies."

And then they were gone, following in a single file line behind Teacher Heather to a door in the back of the sanctuary, along with all the other kids in the congregation.

Sara turned to Owen. He was sitting there, his gaze on the door Janey had disappeared through, his vaguely shadowed jaw completely slack, his shoulders slumped slightly. He looked a bit lost and a little bit upset.

Empathy welled in Sara. Given that she herself hadn't known that kind of devotion or concern from her own dad, and hadn't seen one shred of it in Josh, either, she didn't think there was anything more appealing in a real man.

In fact, the one sitting next to her was turning out to be perfect in just about every way.

Trying to ignore the implications of her realization, she steadied herself and focused on the conversation at hand. "It's hard to let them be independent, isn't it?" she said, taking his hand before she could think better of it.

He froze, his grip rigid with what seemed like surprise. Then, after a long moment, just as she was going to pull her hand away and apologize for touching him, he slowly tightened his fingers around hers, engulfing her hand in a strength and warmth that she hadn't felt from another person in a long time.

He made a rueful sound in the back of his throat. "Not very manly, is it?"

"I think it's wonderful," she replied truthfully. "You care passionately about your daughter. What's better than that?"

He squeezed her hand even tighter and looked into her eyes, his deep blue gaze alight with tender gratefulness. "Thank you," he said softly. "You always seem to know what to say to make me feel better."

His words caused an odd combination of giddiness and warmth to settle like a ball of goo in her chest. She tried to keep herself from falling into the compelling pull of his gaze, tried to speak. But for that small beat of time, she couldn't, and he didn't look away, either.

The organ rang out with the grand beginning chords of the presermon hymn, and the notes bellowing forth from the pipes knocked some much-needed sense into Sara. She dragged her attention away from Owen, reminding herself this was not the time nor the place to get all googly-eyed over him. In fact, she ruthlessly hammered home, there was never a time or place for that reaction. Not anymore.

From the pulpit, Pastor Jacobson asked everybody to rise. Sara stood just as Owen did, and she forced her eyes front and center, trying to keep her focus on the service and off Owen. They were in church, not on a *date*.

But now that she'd seen more of the kind of dad and man he was proving himself to be, she knew without a doubt that keeping him in the just-friends-because-our-daughters-are-friends-and-anyway-he's-leaving-town-soon category was going to be harder than she'd thought.

Yep. She definitely had her work cut out for her.

"I thought the service was really nice," Sara said as she walked next to Owen down the freshly shoveled sidewalk in the center of town.

The girls had insisted on a trip to the Town Square to see the Christmas tree again, so he and Sara had decided to walk the few blocks from church since the snow had let up and patches of blue sky peeked out from among the clouds.

Janey tugged on Owen's hand, and he let go so she could

follow Mia and run ahead of him and Sara to look in the toy store window. "You like the music, don't you?"

"I do." Sara scrunched her nose up. "How did you know?"

"I could just tell by the way your face lit up whenever it started." In fact, he'd barely been able to keep his eyes off her during the service. There was just something so compelling about the way she approached worship, so eagerly and openly, with her whole heart and attention.

Actually, he'd learned in the past few days that there were a lot of compelling things about her, not the least of which was the wonderful way she cared for Mia and Janey. And, of course, how she always seemed to make him feel better with her words of wisdom, as she'd done earlier when he'd had such a hard time letting Janey leave for Sunday school.

Sara turned a lovely smile his way that zinged him right in the gut. "Really? I didn't know my love for the musical part of the worship was so obvious."

Add that knockout smile to the list. "Well, it was." He'd had to remind himself several times that he was here to worship the Lord, not stare at Sara or obsess over how his heart had felt as if it was going to flip right out of his chest when she'd taken a hold of his hand, and when they'd locked gazes. What was wrong with him, anyway? He'd have to get a handle on those reactions.

"Hm. Well, I do love to sing my praise," she said, adjusting the fluffy cream-colored scarf around her neck. "There's something about voices raised together while the organ plays its majestic tones that really touches me and somehow strengthens my bond with God."

"Your faith is strong, isn't it?" he said. One more thing to admire.

"Yes, it is," she replied. "God helped me get through a lot."

"Your divorce?" he ventured after a moment. "Must've been rough."

"Yeah." She looked down for a moment, her jaw visibly

tight, then began to fiddle with the long strands of dark hair tumbling around her shoulders from beneath the cream-colored chunky knit hat she wore. "My ex-husband decided that he didn't want to be a dad when I was a week away from delivering Mia."

Owen's gut rolled and his hands clenched inside his leather gloves. "I won't even tell you what word comes to mind when I hear stuff like that."

She gave him a sideways look. "Why don't you want to tell me?"

"Because the man, for all of his sins, is still Mia's father, and it's not my place to badmouth him," he said from between clenched teeth.

"Really?" she asked.

He jerked his chin to the left and then the right, trying to relax his tight neck muscles. "Really." Guess he better hope to never meet the selfish idiot who'd left Sara and Mia behind.

She stopped in her tracks, blinking.

"What?" he said.

"You sound so…protective."

"I tend to get riled up when women, children or animals are treated poorly."

Her face softened. "So I guess it's good that Josh is re-married to a woman from Germany and never plans to come back?"

"Real good," Owen said, tugging on her hand to get her moving again. After a moment, his curiosity got the better of him. "So you moved back to town after your husband… um, walked out?"

Her mouth tightened as she looked at the ground for a second. "Yes. I grew up here but went to college in California for the good weather, of all things. I met Josh my senior year, we were married a year later, and Mia came along a year after that." She sucked in a shaky breath. "But Josh decided fatherhood wasn't his thing. After he took off, I lived on small nest egg for about six months, and then, when I inherited the bed-and-breakfast from my aunt, I moved back here to run the business and raise Mia."

"So you've been back for about two and a half years?"

"Yes, that'd be about right."

He drew his brows together. "I'm surprised we haven't run into each other more."

"What with being a single mom, and running the B and B, I don't get out much." She gave him a small smile. "And we've already determined we go to different church services."

"True, and I don't get out much, either," he said. Truth was, he'd deliberately kept to himself as he'd dealt with his grief, feeling the need to protect his heart at all costs.

They caught up with the girls at Toys and Trinkets.

Janey turned radiant eyes toward him. "Look, Daddy," she said, pointing in the window. "Animals!"

Sure enough, one wall of the place was packed to the gills with stuffed animals of every kind. "Pretty cool." Smiling, he looked at Sara. "We already have a whole zoo's worth of stuffed animals at home."

"You can never have enough," she replied with a mock seriousness he found, well, completely captivating.

Of course, the girls insisted on going inside, and they spent quite a while in the store admiring just about every stuffed animal ever created.

Owen watched as Sara crouched down to look at each animal Janey and Mia held out, coming up with funny a comment and compliment for each one, even the neon yellow dinosaur with purple buggy eyes and red scales that Owen thought was just plain ugly.

He stood, transfixed, as she put her arm around Janey to discuss what, apparently, was a particularly beautiful horse with a long flowing gold mane and tail. Sara pointed at something on the horse and then bent in and whispered something in Janey's ear that elicited a giggle from his daughter. She nodded and whispered back in Sara's ear. A heartbeat later, Sara laughed and hugged his daughter tight.

Janey looked at him over Sara's shoulder, her eyes alight with pure happiness and contentment and sense of rightness he'd never seen before. And no matter how much he knew he shouldn't assume too much from the touching scene unfolding in front of him, he simply couldn't look away, couldn't help but think that he'd found something very special in Sara Kincaid, something he needed to pay attention to.

But he was leaving town soon. Everything was set up, planned and taken care of. He couldn't change course now.

Even so, going back to where he'd stood just a few weeks ago, before he'd met Sara, was going to be one of the most challenging things he'd ever done.

"Mama, look!" Mia pointed to the window of The Snowglobe Gift Shoppe. "Puppies!"

Sara looked in the window and saw a large brown dog with floppy ears and big black eyes nursing her four chubby puppies. They were tiny, probably under a week old. "Aren't they just adorable?"

"Cute!" Janey said, pressing her face to the window. "Can we pet them?"

"Yeah! I wanna hold one," Mia said.

"They're too young," Owen said. "They need to get older before they'll be ready for touching."

"Oh," both girls said in unison.

Sara stood there with the girls and Owen, commenting on the puppies. Mia liked the brown one, and Janey preferred the black one with spots on its back. Both Mia and Janey just about went nuts when one of the puppies crawled a few feet and fell asleep on its back with all four paws in the air.

After a good five minutes of puppy viewing and exclamations of awe at their cuteness, several people came up be hind Sara's little group. "Girls," she said. "Let's go in and let someone else have a chance to see the puppies."

"Okay," Mia replied, waving. "Bye puppies."

Janey mimicked her. "Yeah. Bye-bye dog babies."

Owen opened the door to the shop, and Sara followed Janey and Mia in. Sara glanced around, and right off, one particular snowglobe sitting on a shelf in the corner jumped out at Sara as if it was lit from within.

Her breath caught. Could it be…?

Before she went over to see if the snowglobe was as personally significant as she thought it might be, she said to Mia and Janey, "Now, remember girls, hands behind your backs so you can lean in and see better." Sara clasped her own hands behind her and, to demonstrate, leaned down and looked pointedly at a giant Christmas-themed snowglobe sitting front and center in the store. "See?"

Eyes wide, Mia and Janey both imitated her.

"Good job," Sara said. "Keep them there, please, my little darlings."

Owen slanted a glance at her, his brows raised in question.

"My mom always used to have me do this to make sure I didn't touch anything fragile," she said by way of an explanation.

"Ah, I see," he said, adopting the same pose. "Very smart."

"A mom's gotta be smart while she's in a place full of fragile stuff," Sara said. "Especially with two curious three-year-olds in tow."

Owen nodded as he took off his gloves and shoved them into his coat pocket. "Good point."

With a look to the girls to be sure they weren't touching anything, Sara hurried over to see the snowglobe she had her eye on, holding her breath just a teensy bit in anticipation of what she would find.

As she drew closer to the display in the corner, she saw that, sure enough, inside the glass globe was a dazzling prancing black horse with a gold bridle and saddle and a long flowing black mane studded with tiny gold jewels. The base was made of intricately carved dark wood, also studded in gold, and if she were correct, the snowglobe would play the song "The Impossible Dream."

Shaking just a bit, she reached for the snowglobe, then lowered her hands for a second to steady them—the last thing she wanted to do was drop something so special. She took the snowglobe off the shelf and felt underneath for the small metal winder. With a twist of her fingers, she wound the music box up and then turned the snowglobe upright.

Familiar music played, soft and melodious, as snow fell down around the black horse, making it look as if the horse was galloping through fluffy snowdrifts. Instantly, precious memories of her mom surrounded her, and her eyes burned. She dipped her head and let the music flow over her, let the memories swirl through her mind, soft and comforting, even as a sadness, muted by time but never gone, wrapped around her heart.

Oh, I miss you so much, Mom...

Someone squeezed her arm. She turned to see Owen standing next to her, his warm gaze etched with concern.

She looked around. "The girls?"

"Dana Caldwell, the owner, is feeding them cider and cookies up front."

"Great. Leaving them unattended in here probably wouldn't be a good idea," she said, wiping her damp cheeks, feeling a bit funny about being caught acting so maudlin.

"You okay?" he asked, his fingers gently encircling her arm.

She held up the snowglobe as her eyes watered even more. "My mom had one just like this when I was a girl."

His eyes softened even more. "Brings back a lot of memories, then, doesn't it?"

"It does. She collected things with carousel horses, and this one was her favorite." She sighed. "I used to look at it way up on the mantel and admire it from afar. I'd beg my mom to take it down so I could see the horse run through the snow while the music played."

"What happened to it?"

Sara swallowed. "She knew how much I loved it, so she gave it to me when Josh and I got married." She ran a hand over the carvings on the base. "When I moved back here, I packed everything up myself, and it broke in transit."

"Oh, wow." He looked at the snowglobe, then held out his hands. "May I?"

She handed it to him, and he gingerly turned it over and made the snow fly around the horse. He gazed at it for a long moment. "So this is pretty special to you."

"Very." She blinked tears away. "Mom died in a car accident right before I got pregnant with Mia."

"I'm so sorry." He reached out and squeezed her arm, his eyes glowing with empathy. "Have you ever thought about replacing it?"

"I have. But unfortunately, it's part of a limited collection, so it's way out of my price range right now." Actually, the way business at the bed-and-breakfast was going, owning another snowglobe like this one would be out of her price range forever.

"Mama, Mama, come look!" Mia called from the front of the store.

Sara gazed longingly at the snowglobe for a few moments and then ran a finger over the glass, trying to imprint the image of the beautiful black horse running in the glittering snow on her memory, and hence, forever remember her mom and the things that were important to her. It was all Sara had left of the woman who, as a single mom, had worked two jobs and sacrificed so much for Sara when she'd been growing up.

"You go," Owen said. "I'll put it back."

Nodding, Sara turned to head up front, feeling the loss

of her mother as if it had just happened yesterday instead of three years ago.

And it hit Sara then and there that having no family to speak of except Mia was a lonely, isolated state indeed. Was she prepared to deal with that for the rest of her life? And perhaps more importantly, why did the status quo suddenly seem so unbearable, so depressing? So not what she wanted?

She shook her head to clear her mind. Why in the world was she so full of big questions today?

She looked upward. *God, I'm going to need some help in the coming days.*

With a turn of her head, she slid a glance back at Owen. Her chest did a cartwheel, and just like that she knew that her dose of self-inquiry was because of a man who had dark blue eyes, broad, capable shoulders, a father's caring heart and a mile wide considerate streak that never failed to knock her out at the knees.

All while making her heart melt away as quickly as her once-strong fears of letting herself love a man again faded away.

Actually, lots of help, Lord.

Chapter Six

"They both conked out on Mia's bed while I was reading them a story," Sara said from the kitchen doorway an hour after they'd all returned to Sara's house for a late lunch. "Guess the adventures of *The Little Drummer Boy* will have to wait until another day."

Owen looked up at her from the dish he was drying, appreciating that she shared his love of reading to Janey. "I guess all of that Christmas fun in town was really tiring." Though he felt energized. Alive. Happy. Maybe he was noticing that now because he hadn't felt so upbeat in a long time?

"Guess so," she said, moving closer. "For Janey, especially. Throwing a fit on Santa's lap has to be exhausting."

He shook his head ruefully. "She really made a scene, didn't she?"

Sara shrugged. "Who cares? I totally understand why she freaked out." Sara grabbed a sponge from the drain board and started wiping off the counters. "I was petrified of the large man with the white hair, long beard and funny red outfit when I was her age, and after one traumatic visit where I probably made him go deaf from my shrieks of horror, I never wanted to go near him again."

He liked how she was trying to ease his embarrassment.

And her strategy was working. Remarkable how she always managed to calm him down and lessen his worries. "So I guess I need to chill and not stress about her Santa fears?"

Sara put the sponge down. "I screamed bloody murder, and the whole town knew it. But my mom took it all in stride, stayed unflappable and never pushed the issue or reminded me about the scene I made."

"She sounds like she was a wonderful woman." Like her daughter.

"She was," Sara replied softly with a wistful smile. "She was the best mom in the world."

"Then that's where you get your fantastic maternal skills," he said, grabbing another dish to dry. "Come by honestly, I'd say. Your mom would be proud."

Sara's face morphed into an appreciative, radiant smile that warmed him up inside like…well, nothing he'd seen in a very long time. "Aw, that's the sweetest thing anyone has ever said to me. Compliments to my mom mean a lot to me."

"Well, I'm not just shooting sunbeams at you. What I said is true." He put the dish in the cupboard, then reached for another. "I really admire how you interact with the girls." Along with a lot of other things, too. She was a special woman, no doubt about it.

"Well, thanks again," she said. "Careful with the compliments, though."

He gave her a questioning stare.

"I might get a big head."

"You? Nope. Never." She didn't seem to have an egotistical bone in her body.

I'm going to miss her.

For the first time, the thought of not having Sara and Mia in his and Janey's lives truly bothered him. Funny how he'd come to look forward to spending time with them. Laughing. Talking. Having fun with the girls.

Worshipping.

Especially that. Just having Sara by his side at church today had been wonderful. He'd missed sharing his faith with someone on a deeper level than simply shaking their hand in the church foyer after the service. Somehow, now that he'd met Sara, the life he'd chosen in Moonlight Cove stretched before him like a blank slate, rather than the rosy picture of starting over somewhere else that had always formed in his mind.

"Owen?" She jiggled his elbow. "You all right?"

"What? Oh, yeah, fine," he replied.

"Since the girls are asleep, you want to go in and sit by the fire with me?" She rubbed her upper arms. "I'm still a bit chilled from walking around town."

"Sounds great," he said. Although he wasn't feeling chilled at all. Had to be the oven-warmed kitchen that had him feeling all toasty. "I can't remember the last time I relaxed in front of a fire with another adult." Much less an attractive, fascinating woman like Sara. Warning flags whipped in his mind, but he did his best to smother the flapping.

"Me, neither," she said, heading out of the kitchen. "It'll be nice to decompress a bit while the girls are asleep. As single parents, we don't get a whole lot of down time."

"No kidding. Between work, Janey and running the household, I don't relax much." Just the thought of figuratively—and literally—putting his feet up for a while sounded great. That in itself was enough to have him agreeing to Sara's offer.

And, really, what was the harm in talking? Just words exchanged, right? No biggie. No commitment, no promises.

He followed Sara into the living room, amazed at how comfortable he felt with her, as if he'd known her for a very long time rather than a bit more than a week. If someone had told him two weeks ago that he'd be hanging out with a pretty young mom by a crackling fire and glowing Christmas tree, he'd have said they were full of beans.

Sara settled on the couch directly across from the fire and next to the lit Christmas tree, her gaze fastened on the flames. He sat down on the same couch—close, but not too close—and leaned back, stretching his upper back and shoulders, feeling a bit tight as he always did on the Sundays he routinely took off from work.

Surprisingly, when he relaxed, he had to resist the sudden urge to put his arm around her and enjoy the fire the way it was supposed to be enjoyed—cuddled up with someone special. Especially since he'd had her in his arms in the sleigh and knew what he was missing now.

Instead, he turned away from that tempting thought and kept his arm to himself…only to feel a bit hollow in his aloneness. Kind of numb inside. He hadn't realized until just now that he'd missed that warm and cozy feeling he got when he pulled a woman close.

However, despite the potential cozy factor, they were just talking here, nothing more, and he couldn't forget that. He had the next part of his life carefully planned out, and those plans didn't include a wonderful hazel-eyed brunette.

It made no sense to let down his guard, he told himself rationally, or give in to his attraction to Sara. He was all about being smart. Keeping his heart to himself. Except with Janey, of course.

"I had a really great time today," Sara said, yanking him from his swirling thoughts. "The girls are at that age where Christmas gets really fun."

"Yeah," he said, admiring her pretty profile. "Did you see their faces when they saw the reindeer?" John Blake, a local rancher who raised reindeer, had brought some of his herd into town as part of the ongoing Snowglobe Christmas festival.

"I thought Janey's eyes were going to pop out of her head," Sara said with a grin that made her eyes crinkle. "She spent a lot of time looking for the one with the red nose, until you told her that Rudolph had stayed home to rest up for Christmas Eve."

"Luckily, that did the trick. She found the one she was sure was Donner, instead, and she was happy."

"Mia immediately identified the one she was sure was Comet." Sara toed off her shoes, exposing fluffy bright red-and-white striped socks, and then tucked her feet up underneath herself, moving a bit closer in the process. "It's amazing how they already know the names of all of Santa's reindeer."

"Did you watch *Rudolph* when you were growing up?" he asked, turning more fully in her direction as he sank a bit more into the crease of the couch cushions.

"Oh, yeah. It's still my favorite movie," she said, chuckling. "Which is probably why Mia already knows all of the reindeer's names."

"I loved it at a kid, too, and bought it on DVD when Janey was born," he replied with his own answering chuckle. "Somehow it just isn't Christmas without watching that movie."

"We should all watch it together." After a second of thought, Sara's eyes grew ever-so-slightly misty. "I always used to love watching it with my mom when I was growing up."

"Sounds like you and your mom were close."

She paused, then drew in a hitchy breath. "We were."

"What about your dad?"

A muscle ticked in her jaw. "He left when I was twelve, and I haven't seen him since." Her voice lacked any tone or inflection at all, but instead of sounding flat and emotionless, it sounded as frozen as the streets outside Sara's door. As if she were clamping down on her emotions and holding something—or a lot of things—in. It spoke volumes. In fact, her tone shot directly to his heart, landing a sympathy-tinged blow that made him wince inside.

He instinctually reached for her hand. "Oh, man, I'm sorry. I didn't know."

She gripped his fingers hard. "Guess it's a sore subject with me." With her free hand she began scraping at the seam on her pant leg. After a few moments of silence, she turned and gave him a wobbly half smile, half grimace that didn't make it to her eyes. "Sad, isn't it, that none of the men in my life seem to want to hang around," she stated.

And I'm one of them.

That thought made his chest implode. He put his arm around her and pulled her close, needing to comfort her as he knew she would comfort him. "Their loss," he said, emphasis on the first word. And his, too?

She nodded against his shoulder, and her soft, citrusy scent floated up to his nose. He fought the urge to breathe deep, needing to stay focused on their conversation rather than on how good she smelled.

"I know that in my head," she whispered, her voice slightly hoarse.

He pulled away very slightly to look at her. "I sense a 'but' coming."

Tears glimmered in her eyes. She looked away, smoothing her dark hair behind one ear. "But in my heart, it just hurts."

Empathy flooded him. "I'm familiar with that heart hurting feeling," he said, stroking her velvety soft cheek. "My heart has been wounded since the day Kristy got her diagnosis." The words came out without hesitation, which belatedly surprised him. He hadn't talked to anyone about Kristy since she'd died—hadn't been able to, actually. What did that say about his relationship with Sara?

Sara reached up and covered his hand on her face with her own much smaller one. Her eyes glowed with understanding, revealing another facet of a bond he was just beginning to understand…and appreciate.

"You know loss, don't you?" she whispered.

"Better than I ever wanted to," he said, leaning back and taking her with him so she was pressed against his side. "Guess we have that in common, don't we?"

She snuggled closer, and he was amazed how right it felt to have her there. "Unfortunately, yes."

He squeezed her shoulder. "You think it's unfortunate that we have something in common?" he gently teased, playing up the double meaning in her statement.

She sat up and gave him an exaggerated stern look. "Ahem. What I meant was, it's unfortunate that we both have had to deal with loss, and, hence, have it in common."

"I knew what you meant. I just like giving you a hard time," he said for some much-needed levity.

She smiled at him sideways, her eyes glinting—but not with tears anymore—then she playfully socked his shoulder. "Trying to tease me, are you?"

"Who? Me?" he said, all mock-innocence. "I'm not the teasing type."

"Ha! You are, too, and you can't backpedal now." She lifted her chin, a smug yet completely adorable look blossoming on her face. "Well, you know what they say about boys who tease girls."

Man, she was cute. "No, enlighten me."

"They say that they only tease the girls they like," she said with a flirty look that spoke to every masculine cell in his body. And every shred of brutal honesty in him. That combination really packed a punch he couldn't ignore if he were to stay sincere. And with Sara, being sincere, he realized, was essential; he respected her too much to not be frank, and he needed to apply that thinking to himself, too.

"Is that so?" he said, sitting up. Gently, he reached up to smooth a hand through her silky hair. "And what if I do like you?" Holding back seemed as impossible as not breathing.

She froze, her teasing smile fading, but she didn't pull away. After a long moment, she swallowed. "Then I'd have to say I'm scared to death."

Locking gazes with her—he couldn't look away now if his life depended on it—he said, "Me, too." Something else they had in common. Another bond. Another thing that made it hard to be careful with his emotions.

Silence descended and she moved closer, then he laid his hands on her shoulders and gently pulled her toward him.

Her hands landed on his chest, and then her lips touched his, softly yet firmly and perfectly. He put his arms around her slim shoulders and settled her against him as he kissed her back.

A feeling of completeness slid down around him like a soft blanket on a cold winter's night.

A moment later, she pulled away slightly, and he had to fight the urge to object. Luckily, she didn't go too far and stayed within touching distance.

"I...didn't expect that," she said, her voice sounding kind of breathless.

"Me, neither." He wasn't going to start lying now. What was the sense in that?

"Are we being foolish?"

Not surprising a levelheaded woman like Sara would have this question, so he took it in stride. "Maybe." He reached out and grasped her hand. "But maybe not."

She blinked but remained silent, nodding slightly.

He took her body language as an invitation to go on. "We're both essentially doing the single parent thing right now, and Mia and Janey love each other. What's the harm in spending a bit of time together?" The words *before I leave town* hovered in the air.

Chewing on her lip, her shoulders tense, Sara took in what he was saying with open ears, contemplating his rationale. Yes, she wanted to depend on no one but herself. But she knew the score with Owen up front, knew he wasn't going to be sticking around, so she wouldn't expect anything from him. In a twisted way, that made things easier; she wouldn't be getting her hopes up for more. Easy. As long as she didn't let herself fall for him, she'd be fine. And really, she wanted so badly to spend time with another adult. Especially someone as cute and as interesting as Owen...

She cut that errant thought off and focused on answering him. "I guess it wouldn't hurt to enjoy the fire together." And more, emotionally? Nope. She knew better than to get her heart involved and wouldn't forget the lessons her ex and father had taught her.

Owen lifted an arm, crooked an eyebrow at her and grinned. "Then come on over here and let's do this fire some justice."

For some odd reason, the tension in her upper body flowed away. With a glance at his devastating smile, she snuggled down next to him on the couch. He pressed a quick, soft kiss to her head, and her heartbeat skittered. The fire crackled and sputtered, casting fingers of warmth into the room that rivaled the toasty, contented feeling glowing in her heart.

And in that moment, Sara did her best to ignore the small yet insistent voice inside telling her to run away as if the fire had shot out of the fireplace and set her hair ablaze.

Chapter Seven

Sara consulted the ear thermometer. "Well, girls, you both have fevers, so it's into bed for a nice nap."

Pale and noticeably listless, Mia and Janey looked up at Sara, their little shoulders hunched.

"Okay, Mommy," Mia said. "I don't feel good."

Janey chimed in with, "Yeah." She rubbed her eyes. "I so tired."

Sara raised an eyebrow as she popped the cap on the thermometer. They'd both been dragging all morning; they must be pretty sick if they were so willing to go to sleep in the middle of the afternoon.

She knew the feeling. She had a rare headache, and she'd been feeling lethargic and a bit chilled all day long. Maybe she could use a nap, too. Although she had a ton of business paperwork to do and she wasn't the napping type. No time in her life, for sure.

"Okay, let's go get you some medicine, and then we'll hop in bed and make you two cozy," she said with a hand on each of their shoulders.

Bleary-eyed, the girls trudged into the kitchen, where they both dutifully took the liquid children's fever reducer Sara poured for them. Then Sara shepherded them into bed, and they instantly nestled down under the covers, two sad, sick little cherubs laying side by side, off to afternoon dreamland.

Sara adjusted the covers. "You guys just sleep, all right?"

Silence. She craned her neck and saw that both kidlets were already drifting off. Good. Rest was the best medicine. She'd go tell Owen what was up right now.

Owen. Just the thought of him sent her tummy into a spin-out. It had been three days since they'd kissed in the light of the Christmas tree. And while they hadn't kissed again, or spent any more time all alone in front of the fire—or anywhere else—they had spent the evenings together with the girls since the smooch. In fact, they'd all watched *Rudolph, the Red-Nosed Reindeer* last night while they munched on popcorn balls she, Mia and Janey had made yesterday.

But that mind-boggling, toe-curling, fantastic kiss had remained on Sara's mind as if it had just happened five minutes ago. And the truth was, no matter how she approached the subject, she couldn't see any way around the inevitable conclusion she'd made about five this morning as the moon bounced off the snow outside and shined into her bedroom window.

Owen was leaving Snowglobe in a week. There you had it; the be all end all, can't-ignore-reality truth. While he made her feel special and protected and happy and less lonely—which she hadn't even realized was an issue until he'd come into her life—she simply could not let herself get any more emotionally involved with him than she already was.

In fact, she hoped she could return to the status quo after letting herself go to a romantic yet incredibly idealistic place that, while wonderful and warm and toasty, wasn't real or practical. Or, she thought pragmatically, in any way sane.

She made her way toward the back door to tell him Janey and Mia were down for the count with a germ, all the while reminding herself that it was past time to back away from Owen and take care of her heart. She needed to stand on her own.

Just as she opened the door, an unnatural wave of a chill washed over her, and her upper back started to ache. Her head throbbed, and suddenly, she felt really awful. As in…sick.

She pressed a hand to her throbbing head and rolled her shoulders. Great. Looked like the girls had already shared their germs with her. Or, more likely, they'd all picked the bug up at the same time.

Sara didn't have time to be sick. It was just her, taking care of everything. She'd turned powering through no matter what into a necessary and useful art form. She'd gutted out sickness before; she'd do it again out of necessity. Single parents didn't have sick days, or even hours.

Just as she was about to step out onto the patio, Owen showed up at the back door. She stared for just a moment; he looked cuter in his knit hat and work clothes than any man had a right to look. Probably a good thing she didn't feel well, or she might instigate a repeat kiss right here and right now.

Had to be the fever scrambling her good sense.

She opened the door. "Hey. I was just coming out to talk to you."

He peered at her. "Everything okay?"

"Janey and Mia both have fevers, and believe it or not, they're sound asleep right now."

"In the middle of the afternoon?"

"Yep." A wave of achy exhaustion swept through her and she felt her shoulders sag a little.

Owen put his hands on his narrow hips and looked closely at her. After a few beats, he whipped off his right glove and, before Sara could see the tricky move coming, pressed a cool hand to her forehead. His brows slammed together. "You have a fever, too."

"Maybe."

He pressed his hand to her head again, lingering longer.

If she didn't feel so crummy, she'd savor the feeling of his cool hand on her warm skin. Good thing she was ill—or not.

He frowned. "No maybe about it." His eyes zeroed in on her face. "And come to think of it, you don't look well, either."

She gave him a deadpan stare, hoping he'd drop the subject; the last thing she wanted was for him to baby her.

"Don't even try to pull that on me," he said, waving a finger in front of her motionless face. "I'm a dad, and I've been around enough fevers to know when someone has one."

She shrugged. "Okay, so maybe I am feeling a bit feverish."

"I knew it."

She winced as the ache in her upper back spread down and another chill gripped her. "So what? I have too much to do to be sick." Paperwork. Cleaning. Meal prep. Motherhood. As usual, the list was endless.

"It can all wait," he said, taking his other glove off and shooing her to take a step backward into the kitchen. "You need to lie down right now."

She backed up. "No, I don't have time."

He glared at her as he pushed the door closed.

"What if the girls need me?" she asked, chewing on her lip as the idea of a nap beckoned like a wonderful dream.

"I'll take care of the girls," he said, unzipping his coat.

"From the roof?"

His gloves landed on the counter. "I'll stay in here."

She opened her mouth to protest.

"Jeff and I are making good time, and he's perfectly capable of finishing up today on his own."

She crossed her arms over her chest. "I don't do naps," she said, taking another tack, knowing she sounded childish. It had to be the germ talking; she wasn't usually petulant. But she was feeling too blech to care.

"Not even when you're sick?"

"I'm on my own," she said as another throb jolted through her head, followed by a sizzling chill that made her whole body ache. "If I take time out to lie around, nothing gets done."

His face softened. "You're not on your own today," he said, putting his hands on her shoulders, his blue eyes seeking hers. "I'm here, and I can take over. I'll make dinner."

His words lit a small rogue fire inside her chest that had nothing to do with any kind of germ. She pressed her lips together, refusing to meet his gaze. Boy, he was persuasive.

"Sara, look at me."

Reluctantly, she did as he asked, even though she was afraid she'd fall into his eyes and never find herself.

"Would it hurt just this once to lean on someone else?"

His question hit right at the crux of the matter. "I don't like depending on other people. Every time I've done that, with the exception of my mom, I've been left alone and hurting."

"I know, and I can't tell you how what your dad and ex did sticks in my craw." He looked away, his jaw flexing. "But I think in this instance, for your own good, and for the girls, too, you need to get in bed and sleep so you can get well fast and be back on your feet in no time. You look like you're about ready to drop."

A wave of exhaustion rolled over her, pulling at her like taut ropes around her limbs. "Tricky, using the girls as ammunition."

"Not ammunition," he said, shaking his head. "The truth."

He was right; she felt as if her bones were made of lead. In a tiny part of her brain, she wondered what it would be like to have someone take over for her for just a little while so she could sleep. She didn't get many breaks, and with an illness bearing down on her it would be novel to be able to let someone take care of her for a change.

Plus, she was in no shape to be up working. And she *would* recover faster if she took care of herself now. "Guess I should count myself lucky that you're here to take over."

"Well, yeah, that goes without saying," he said, quirking his mouth up at one corner. "I make a pretty good nurse."

"I'm sure you do," she said, meaning it. "I bet you can take a temperature with a smile as well as you swing a hammer or run a band saw." Was there anything this guy couldn't do?

As he turned her around with gentle pressure to her shoulders and she headed to the luxury of the couch in the parlor in the middle of the afternoon, the answer to her own question reverberated through her mind like a shotgun blast.

The only thing the wonderful man in her kitchen couldn't do was stay in Snowglobe forever.

Owen found Sara's list of chores and spent the afternoon doing laundry, mopping the kitchen and foyer floors and cleaning the upstairs bathroom between silently checking on the girls and Sara.

As he worked, and not for the first time, either, he couldn't help but remember every detail of his and Sara's kiss, and he had to fight wanting a repeat. Not a good idea, of course, but his memories of having her close seemed to have a mind of their own.

He also went over their conversation about her dad and ex's desertion as he had more than once since they'd talked. She'd had it rough, no doubt about it, and that tore him up inside. His gut burned every time he thought about it. What a couple of losers. Was it any wonder she didn't want to lean on anyone?

Yeah, she was stubborn, and took her mom and entrepreneur duties very seriously, which impressed him to no end. He could tell it had taken a lot for her to let him take over while she slept; she was used to depending on no one but herself. But in the end, she'd done the right thing, even though it had clearly gone against her instincts. Again, he couldn't help but note she was an exceptional person.

A truly wonderful woman, one he had a feeling he should somehow hang on to, even though that was the last thing he'd thought he wanted. Was it possible he had the rest of his life planned wrong?

And he couldn't deny Mia was good for Jane. His little girl had really come out of the shell she'd been hiding in since Kristy had died, and he knew that he had, in part, the more outgoing Mia to thank for that transformation. All in all, the Kincaid ladies were good for Janey. Really good.

What about for him?

He had no concrete answers, except that it was really weird that he was having so many doubts after being so confident that leaving Snowglobe was the right thing to do before he'd met Sara. Was he really that messed up?

Not a comforting thought.

Just as he'd finished making a scrambled egg and waffle dinner to serve to his patients, the lights flickered. He froze for a moment, plates in hand, waiting. The lights came back on and he gave a sigh of relief, then continued setting the table.

The idea of a power outage ran through his mind as he worked. Maybe he should go dig up a flashlight, just in case?

He methodically went through the kitchen drawers, finding a small flashlight in the last drawer he looked in. Shoving it in his pocket, he continued setting the kitchen table.

Just about the time he had the silverware in place, the lights dimmed, bumped up again…and then went out, leaving him in complete darkness.

Thankful he'd listened to his instincts, he pulled the flashlight out and turned it on. Looked like they were in for an interesting evening. Luckily, he already had dinner made.

Figuring the girls might be scared if they woke up in total darkness, he made his way to Sara's room where Mia and Janey slept, glancing out the front door on the way by. From the looks of the darkened street, most of the town was without power.

He awakened the girls before he roused Sara, making a silly game out of the flashlight casting funny shadows on the wall. Then, with one girl's hand in each of his, and the flashlight clamped between his teeth, he went to get Sara.

She awoke easily, and he quickly explained what was going on. She sprang up and took Janey's hand and they led the girls to the kitchen. Sara found some candles, and they ate dinner by candlelight. Both girls perked up during the meal.

He insisted Sara let him do the dishes, but she, of course, wanted to help, declaring she felt better.

"How long do you think this outage will go on?" she asked as she dried dishes. The girls were playing with their little ponies at the candlelit kitchen table.

"No idea. Could be all night."

She nibbled on her bottom lip. "We'd better get the fire going, then." She glanced out the window at the swirling snow. "It's going to get cold in here."

He paused. "You want me to stay?"

Sara's chin went up. "Nah. We'll be fine." There was that independent streak of hers.

"You sure?"

"Positive." She dried the last dish and put it away. "I'm a big girl."

He gave her an I-know-you-are-but-I'm-still-worried look.

She waved a hand in the air. "Relax, Prince Charming. We're just going to be sleeping."

"Well, at least let me build the fire before we go."

"Okay. I'll give the girls some more acetaminophen while you do that."

Uneasy with the arrangement but wanting to give Sara the space she needed, he wiped the counters and then went in to the living room and started a nice fire. Thinking ahead, he went out and started the truck so it would be warmed up when he and Janey got in.

Then, once he was confident everything was in order, he bundled a sleepy Janey into her coat and hat. Sara still looked like she was dragging, but she assured him she could handle

Mia for the rest of the evening, with or without power, while thanking him for his help.

He waved off her thank-you as nothing big because it wasn't and gave her a quick hug as he told her to take care of herself. With a promise to be back in the morning, and making sure Sara would call if she needed anything, he hustled Janey out to his truck, being careful in the silent darkness. The snow was really coming down, and he hoped it stopped soon or he and Jeff would have to spend a lot of time tomorrow morning clearing the roof before they could get started. Assuming the power was back on by then…

The darkness of the truck's cab wrapped around him as he shifted into four-wheel drive and started home. Truthfully, after his busy day spent at Sara's, he felt a bit alone, especially with no lights on anywhere. His headlights cut a bright swath through the falling snow and the quietness of the night closed in around him. Inevitably his thoughts shifted to Sara, and affection grew in his chest and radiated outward, warming him from the inside out.

"Daddy?" Janey said from her car seat, dragging his thoughts away from Sara's warming effects.

"I thought you were asleep, baby girl."

"No."

"You all right?"

"Uh-huh, 'cept my head hurts a little bit."

"That's because you have a virus."

"Oh."

Silence.

Then from the darkness, "Daddy, I like Sara."

His heart just about stalled as his mind made a one-eighty, right back to Sara. Funny how he'd been doing that particular half circle a lot lately. "I do, too, honey."

"Is she coming wif us when we move?"

"Um…no, she's not," he shoved out, his throat tight. Interesting how the thought of not having Sara by his side in a little over a week made him feel downright sick inside.

"Why not?" Jane asked, her voice small yet full of disbelief that killed him. "I thought we were a fambly."

Her question zapped him like he'd been shocked by a live wire. He pressed a hand to the bridge of his nose. Oh, man. What could he say? Janey was way too young to understand the ins and outs of adult relationships, but he didn't want to make up some lie.

So he settled on a gentle version of the truth. "Honey, Sara is a very nice lady who is my friend and your babysitter."

"Like Mona?" she asked.

Those two words stopped him short, and he resisted the urge to chuckle at his daughter's interpretation of the situation. Funny how little kids saw things in black-and-white, without much gray in between.

Whatever the case, Janey's comment forced him to admit that, no, the way he felt about Sara was not like Mona at all. Mona was a kindly middle-aged woman with grandkids of her own, a heart of gold and a huge soft spot for Janey. All wonderful qualities for sure. But no way had he ever felt the need to spend one-on-one time with Mona as he had with Sara.

In fact, since Kristy had died, he hadn't felt even the slightest urge to be with any woman...

Until Sara.

His mouth went dry.

Shrugging off the significance of his thoughts as best he could, he instead focused on the conversation at hand. "Um... well, kind of like Mona," he replied, settling on a version that wasn't a lie, but was enough to answer Janey's question. "She and Sara are both really nice ladies, aren't they?"

"Uh-huh," Jane said.

For a few long moments, nothing but the sound of the windshield wipers echoed throughout the truck's cabin.

Then Janey said, "But you never hold hands with Mona."

He tightened his grip on the steering wheel, wishing he'd had the foresight not to take Sara's hand in his as they'd walked through town. But what was done was done, no going back. Trouble was, how could he explain the difference between Mona and Sara to Janey in a way she would understand?

"Um…that's because Mona's married," he said, snagging on the only reasoning that was both solid and easy for Janey to understand. "She already loves Elmer, right?"

"Oh. Right," Janey said. "She already had a webbing with him."

He smiled at her mangled pronunciation. "Exactly."

"'Cause she likes Elmer, right?"

"Right," Owen said. Best leave the discussion at that.

"Well, I wish Sara and Mia could come wif us." Silence. "If you like her and I like her, why can't you have a webbing? Mia and me could be flower girls and wear our princess costumes and walk down the mile together. And then we could play together all the time!" Her tone shined with such hope, he could barely draw a full breath.

Words stuck in his throat for a second, leaving a burning lump behind. He was an absolute idiot for letting himself and Janey get so involved with the Kincaid ladies; she was already envisioning herself walking down a church aisle in a pretty dress with her supposed soon-to-be forever playmate.

Well, there was no help for it; he was going to have to be honest. "Because Sara and I don't love each other," he forced out even as the statement burned.

"Why not?" Janey asked.

More honesty needed. "Because I don't want to fall in love again," he said. If he said it enough, it would be true. He'd make sure of it.

"Oh."

He drove in silence for a few moments.

Janey spoke up again. "Daddy?"

"Yes?"

"I think you be sad if you don't have someone to love."

The softly spoken words rammed into him like a hammer strike. What if her proclamation was true?

Shoving that explosive thought away, he said, "As long as I have you, I'll be happy."

"Okay."

But, suddenly, nothing was okay. The pesky lump remained in his throat while Janey's statement bounced around in his brain, refusing to be ignored.

I think you'll be sad if you don't have someone to love.

Was that true? Was he relegating himself to a life of unhappy loneliness by choosing to guard his heart at all costs?

As he looked at the cold winter's night enveloping the truck with snow and freezing temperatures, his confusion over Sara deepened. Quite possibly he would be less happy alone than with Sara and her kind spirit, lilting laugh and compelling presence. But he'd also retain power over what went on in his life. No risk, no pain, no loss. And wasn't that what he'd wanted since Kristy had died?

Yes, yes it was. No other way as far as he could see, not if he wanted to keep things nice and smooth in his life, which he did. Given that, he knew he needed to head things off before they went any further, even though the thought of leaving Snowglobe made his chest ache now that he'd be leaving Sara, as well.

Despite his decision, he couldn't get rid of the nagging notion that he just didn't feel right about leaving Sara and Mia alone and under the weather in a dark, cold house with no power.

Making a snap decision that belied his state of mind, he slowed down and made a careful U-turn in the snow-covered street and headed back to Sara's house.

And sent a prayer up to God that his choice to leave Snowglobe early was the right one for everyone involved.

Chapter Eight

Sara's eyes had about popped out of her head when Owen and Janey had shown back up last night. But her heart had warmed, too, to see him on her doorstep. He really was a thoughtful guy, and his coming all the way back for her meant a lot.

Now it was morning, and the power was still out. Owen had awakened early as he and Sara had planned, and he'd gone home to check on things there and shower with whatever hot water was left in his hot water tank. As decided, he left Janey with Sara and Mia.

Fortunately, Sara felt much better this morning. She still had a shadow of a headache, but the body aches and chills were gone. Time to get on with a normal day.

Mia and Janey seemed to be better, too, and after they ate a no-cook breakfast of cold cereal with bananas, they plopped themselves down in front of the fire to play with their toy ponies, which they'd named Caramel and Latte, after Mr. Ingerson's draft horses.

Sara worked on loading the dishwasher, which she'd run as soon as the power came back on—whenever that would be. Owen had already told her that he and Jeff couldn't work without electricity to run their tools, so the roof job would be put on hold. But given the progress they'd made, she was confident their work would be finished before Owen left town for Moonlight Cove. All the way out on the West Coast. Pacific Northwest to be exact. Pretty, she was sure. Still…they were leaving.

She stopped for a moment as she loaded the dishwasher, afraid she'd drop something, thinking about Owen and how he'd so lovingly and willingly taken over yesterday, and how he'd come back last night.

And how glad she'd been to see him, to know he cared about her enough to stay. Yes, it had felt wonderful to rely on someone else for a bit, to allow herself a break.

To relax.

She missed that feeling, missed having a backup. Truthfully, since she'd had Owen around, she realized how much she missed having a man in her life. Would it be so bad to allow herself to slide back into partner mode?

She took a deep breath and tried not to panic at the stunning course of her thoughts. She had to be honest with herself; she owed herself that, didn't she?

Seeing Owen in action yesterday had simply capped off what she'd already known deep in her heart, though she'd been sidestepping the truth for days. He was a wonderful person, a splendid father and the epitome of everything she admired in a man—steadfast, loving, faithful and kind. Not to mention he was the most handsome man she'd ever run across, and the thought of kissing him again sent sparks through her.

With a gasp she sagged against the counter, then jumped back when water soaked the front of her shirt. She was a mess, in more ways than one!

Feeling shaky, she sat at the table, pressing a hand to her brow. She didn't want him to leave; she wanted both him and Janey in her and Mia's lives. But leaving had always been his plan. Would he change his mind for her? Or maybe they could do the long distance thing…? Surely there was some way to work this out. Because she couldn't leave the B and B, not when she was just beginning to make a success of the place.

She'd be taking a big risk by asking him to stay. But maybe, just maybe, taking a leap of faith was the key to her and Mia's future happiness.

The doorbell rang just then, and her heart started pounding. Owen was back, and she wasn't sure she was ready to clue him in to what she had in mind. But it wasn't like she had a lot of time to dink around the issue; they'd be gone from town in less than a week, and if she didn't speak up now, they wouldn't have any reason to stay.

And suddenly she wanted them to stick around with everything in her.

She took a deep breath and stood, steadying herself for just a moment with a hand on the kitchen table. Nothing worth having was easy to get.

Shoving her chin in the air to at least feel—and look—courageous, she headed out to the foyer to let Owen in. With trembling hands, she unlocked the door and opened it.

As expected, Owen stood on the other side, all decked out in cold weather gear since the skies had cleared some overnight, which had brought a temperature drop to well below freezing.

Feeling as if every single emotion inside of her was evident on her face, Sara forced her expression into what she hoped was a neutral mode and made herself look at Owen, as if she hadn't just decided to spill about her feelings for him.

His broad shoulders drooped just a little, his eyes seemed less bright and his brow was distinctly furrowed. He seemed… sad? Upset? Maybe a little of both?

As she stepped aside to let him in, Sara frowned at his uncharacteristic demeanor. "You okay?"

He unzipped his parka. "Fine," he said, though he said it in a way that didn't seem fine at all.

Sara pushed the door closed, another layer of unease filtering through her, making her even more apprehensive to tell him about her feelings.

He hung his coat on the antique hall tree adjacent to the door, just as he did every time he arrived. The thought of their little routine ending made Sara's chest ache. All the more reason she needed to level with him about what she wanted.

"It makes me sad to think that you won't be working here anymore after you and Jeff finish." Hopefully, though, they'd have a brand-new routine taking shape in their lives very soon. Or maybe not. But she had to open up, even if doing so didn't change anything. He wasn't a mind reader, right?

He turned and then looked at the floor as he slowly took his hat off. "Listen, we need to talk."

Her chest hollowed out. "That sounds ominous."

Avoiding her gaze, he said, "Let's go sit down and talk in the kitchen."

The bottom of her stomach dropped. Obviously there must be something really heavy on his mind. Something about them? It didn't sound like he just had concerns about her roof or anything like that. Maybe she was being sensitive given her new feelings for him, but either way, she had a suspicion this conversation he wanted to have didn't bode well for her. At all.

She cleared her throat. "Okay. I lit the burner on the stove with a match and made instant coffee. Not great, but I have a feeling we're both going to need it."

He pointed to the door. "I forgot something in my truck. I'll meet you in the kitchen."

"All right." As Owen disappeared out the door, she forced herself to be pragmatic about their upcoming conversation. What other choice did she have? She couldn't exactly cover her ears and sing "The Star Spangled Banner" to drown out what he was going to lay on her. She had to deal with whatever Owen had on his mind.

Though she had a feeling she was going to wish she'd

sung her heart out before he had the chance to *yank* it out with what he was about to tell her.

Owen entered the empty kitchen and immediately noticed two matching mugs on the counter, one for Sara and, presumably, one for him. His eyes went back and forth between the twin mugs, the significance of their presence not lost on him. Already he was part of Sara's routine.

His belly tanked and sent tendrils of fire into his upper body. While on the one hand he liked that she was always thinking of him, on the other, her including him in her morning coffee ritual scared him.

He puffed out a large breath, then poured himself a big cup of java and resisted the urge to gulp the hot liquid down. No sense in having a burned throat to go along with the flaming lump of panic forming in his chest.

Finally, he took a tentative sip of coffee, reiterating to himself as he did so that he was doing the right thing by leaving town early and cutting off what was going on with him and Sara before their relationship went any deeper. Sara's roof was almost done, and Jeff was going to finish up the one other job Owen had on his schedule.

John Ruppello had been thrilled to have Owen show up in Moonlight Cove a week early since they had a new client who wanted a rush job, so that end was covered. No reason to hang around, even for another week. He had the flight to Seattle booked for later tonight, and the property management company handling the details on the rental of his house was going to be putting up a For Rent sign later today. He had a call into the moving company to cover last-minute details.

Everything was ready.

He rubbed the bridge of his nose. Now he had to tell Sara they were leaving.

Just as he was sitting down at the small table in the corner, she came through the door that led to the garage carry ing a package of frozen chicken. She had furrow lines in her normally smooth forehead.

Undoubtedly she had an inkling of what was on the horizon, realizing that "we need to talk" usually didn't promise hearts and Cupid's arrows. Unfortunately, that notion held true now. Hearts and Cupid's arrows just didn't fit in with what he wanted. Or rather, with what he could allow.

Without a word, she set the chicken on the counter to thaw and then poured herself a cup of coffee. She took a sip, then stood with her hip propped against the counter. "So, what did you want to talk about?"

"Um…you want to sit down?" he said, gesturing to the chair opposite him.

She raised her chin and slanted him a glance. "I'll stand." Her voice held a distance that landed a gut-punch worthy of Joe Frazier.

He winced. She had her shields up. Not surprising, really, but pretty disconcerting just the same; having Sara act this distant was like eating glass. Guess that was a necessary casualty of the situation. Hopefully, he'd recover. Eventually. "Okay." He took another sip of coffee. "So…um, I have some news."

"Go on," she said, nodding.

"Well…" He swallowed. "I've decided to leave town a bit earlier than originally planned." Why did that sound so lame said out loud?

Her shoulders sagged just a teensy bit. "Why?"

He forced himself to say, "I've always planned on leaving Snowglobe." He'd made that clear.

"No, why are you leaving early?" she asked in an overly even voice, as if she were forcing herself to stay level.

He opened his mouth to speak—to say something, anything. But what? More lameness? He rubbed the back of his neck.

She spoke before he could say anything. "You're running away."

He blinked. "Not really—"

"Yes, really." She started to pace. "You're scared to death of what's happening with us, and this is your way of escaping the truth."

"What truth is that?" he asked, his heart skipping a beat.

"That we've formed a connection over the last week," she whispered.

His mouth went dry.

She continued on. "We kissed, Owen. And I want to do it again. That has to mean something, doesn't it?"

Her statement sent happiness soaring through him for a moment. But he killed the giddiness and forced it to die an efficient death. A *connection* was a threat he had to avoid to keep his life on an even keel, within the parameters he'd set when Kristy died and his world had fallen apart. No matter what, no matter the possible reward.

"What it means is that we're attracted to each other. I really like you, Sara. But I'm not ready to move beyond that. I don't think I'll ever be ready."

She closed her eyes for a moment and her lips quivered.

"Are *you* ready for more?" he asked before he could think better of the question, almost afraid to hear her answer. Thinking about walking away from her was one thing; actually doing it with her standing there looking so vulnerable, so achingly sad, was a whole 'nother kettle of fish. One that involved shoving aside what he wanted to do in the short run to protect the long run.

She paused for a significant moment, then her brow smoothed out and her shoulders straightened. "Yes." She nodded. "Yes, I am."

Surprise zinged through him like a shot, along with an unmistakable sense of pleasure he had no business feeling. "Really?"

She moved over next to him and put her hand on his shoulder. "Yes, Owen, really. I've realized in the last few days that I like having someone to lean on." She gave him a look so full of hope he almost had to turn away. "That someone would be you."

His heart seized.

She gave him a shaky smile. "I think we have something here, something special. I'm asking you to stay in Snowglobe. Stay with me and Mia, give us a chance."

He sank back in his chair. Something akin to terror wound around his chest, cutting off his breath, forcing him to say, "Sara, I…I can't."

With a small sound of dismay, she sat down in the chair opposite him.

He pressed on, forcing himself to be honest with her. What other choice did he have? They were talking about their futures here; now was not the time to pull any punches. Or stuff the truth. He respected her too much to play games.

"This is what my gut is telling me to do and I don't see any way around it." He looked right at her. "Let me ask you this, to put things in perspective. Would you be willing to move to Moonlight Cove?"

She stilled, her jaw rigid. "I have a business here."

"So the answer is no?"

She blinked several times but remained quiet.

"I can see the truth," he said. "You want to avoid love as much as I do."

Her jaw visibly tightened. "You realize, don't you, what we might have here?"

Hopeless possibilities danced through his head: he and Sara and the girls as a family, Sara by his side forever, all the fabulous things a loving relationship entailed. A tempting picture for sure. But his gut level needs trumped the appealing picture. "Definitely. You're a wonderful woman, Sara.

In another place and time, you would be exactly the kind of person I'd be looking for."

"Well, that makes me feel better," she said with a quick twist of her lips.

He cringed inwardly. He was making a mess of this. "Maybe that came out wrong." He rubbed his cheek. "What I mean is that my leaving isn't about you. It's about me and what I want in my life."

"Which is?"

"To not get hurt again by losing someone."

"You mean you want control."

He canted his head to the side. "I guess so."

"You think I don't want control?" She laughed without humor. "I know it's scary to put your heart on the line, to let your emotions rule your head. But don't you think the ultimate reward is worth it? Don't you think trusting in God's plan is the right thing to do?"

"Maybe for some people. But not for me. I can't let myself lose someone I love again. I just can't, and I have to stop things now before the risk of pain is too great. Maybe that instinct is a sign that what I'm doing *is* God's plan for me."

"But you're losing me now," she said softly, taking his hand. "Doesn't that count?"

As his heart jerked in his chest, he stared at their two hands twined together. Those agonizing possibilities taunted him. "Of course it does," he said. "But I can control this loss before my life takes a turn I *can't* control."

"So as long as you consciously choose it, loss is okay?"

He thought about that concept for a moment. Sounded crazy. But true. "Yes, because I get to choose rather than having something decided for me."

She let go of his hand, and he felt the loss of her touch clear to the soles of his work boots.

Going on, she said, "Has it ever occurred to you that by letting that happen, you're in truth relinquishing any power you ever had over your life in the first place? Any faith that God's plan is the right one?"

His jaw sagged as the truth in her words rammed into him. "You're right."

"I sense a *but* here," she said.

"*But,* your reasoning, while sound, doesn't make a difference for me. I have to be comfortable with the risks I take with my life, at what I let God handle for me."

"And I'm not one of the comfortable risks, right?" she asked, her voice coated in what distinctly sounded like hurt.

"I'm sorry," he said with all the honesty he could muster. "I have to do this." It wouldn't be fair to give either himself or Sara false hope.

She stood. "I think you're making a big mistake," she said.

Worry shot through him. "You might be right about that, and I might look back on this decision and regret it. But hindsight is twenty-twenty, and I don't have that right now. I can only go with my gut here and do what I think is best for me. And right now, going to Moonlight Cove is what I have to do." Now, more than ever, he needed a fresh start, away from the painful memories that seemed to permeate his life in Snowglobe.

She blinked quickly several times and then took a deep breath. After a moment where she seemed to be steadying herself—and her emotions—she turned away.

He almost called out, but he bit the words off.

She turned to him, concern etched into her lovely features. "What are we going to tell the girls?"

Figured she'd be thinking of Janey and Mia; she always had their best interests at heart.

"The truth, I guess," he said. "Janey knows we're moving."

"I'm worried they're going to be upset," Sara replied, chewing on her lower lip. "They've really bonded."

The girls had become inseparable over the past week, and

it was hard for him to sever that connection. "As long as you and I are there for them, they'll be fine."

Owen belatedly flinched; the words *you and I* held a hollow echo of what could have been in another life with another set of circumstances.

"I hope so," Sara replied, frowning. "I'm sure Mia is going to be wondering where Janey is in the morning."

What could he say to that? She was right. "I'm sorry this is the way it has to be."

He swallowed past the burning lump in his throat. "And please know that Jeff will be here to finish the roof as soon as the power goes back on."

"Okay." Sara paused, then pressed her lips together. "If you ever need anything, anything at all, please don't hesitate to call. No matter what happens, I will always care about you and Janey, more than you'll ever know."

And then, with a terse nod, Sara turned and left the kitchen, nothing but the clicking of her heels on the hardwood floors echoing in her wake.

Owen sat there, alone, once again thinking what a truly extraordinary person Sara was, and that she obviously possessed a true and gracious heart. Pretty amazing.

Regret and grief for his loss pounced on him in a stranglehold, sending searing pain into his chest. He pressed a hand to the aching place over his heart, hoping and praying his sorrow and regret was short-lived and manageable and that he hadn't just made the biggest mistake of his life.

Chapter Nine

From the porch, Sara watched Owen and Janey drive off as the snow silently fell to the ground in a blanket of white shadowed with gray. The truck's taillights faded into the fuzzy distance as he turned the corner a block away and disappeared from view. Forever.

Why was this scenario such a pattern in her life? Why did she always seem to be watching men she loved walk away?

Tears formed in her eyes and her throat burned. Saying goodbye to Owen and Janey without completely breaking down had been the hardest thing Sara had ever done. But she'd kept a concrete upper and lower lip for the girls' sake, and for Owen, too. He'd made his decision, and he was entitled to that choice without having to deal with any kind of emotional reaction on her part. Just as she was entitled to her own choice. And she chose…to stay here.

Even if her heart was crumbling, leaving a gaping hole in her chest. Even if she thought he was blinded to a bright future by the traumatic loss he'd suffered in the past, that he wasn't trusting in God's plan. But what choice did she have but to honor Owen's decision?

Maybe it was better this way; life would go on, and her heart would stay safe. Small comfort. Minuscule, actually, but it was all she had to keep herself from breaking down completely.

Sara plodded through the rest of the morning and afternoon, determined to keep her pain at bay with busy work that could be done without electricity. Mia faded late in the afternoon and conked out on the couch while Sara read her a *My Little Pony* story by the window in the parlor.

Weary and heartsick and mentally spent, Sara laid down next to her little girl, pulled a blanket over the both of them and closed her eyes. Within moments, the blessed oblivion of sleep claimed her.

Sara awoke with a start after dreaming of a wedding starring her as the bride, Mia and Janey as twin flower girls and a certain blue-eyed man as the groom waiting for her at the end of the church aisle as Jesus looked down from the cross behind the altar.

She sat up, careful not to disturb Mia, sad to realize the wedding was just a dream and nowhere near the reality Owen had slammed home a few hours earlier.

Pushing her hair out of her eyes, Sara sat for a moment, her heart aching, gearing up to get on with her day. Owen was gone, but life went on. She supposed.

As she stood, she turned on the flashlight she'd set on the coffee table, sweeping its beam up. Instantly, her gaze snagged on a gift tucked under the tree. Odd. She hadn't put the present there; in fact, she was monstrously behind on Christmas stuff and hadn't wrapped one gift yet. Curious, she went over and picked the gaily wrapped box up, noting it was heavy for its size.

There was a card tucked under the pretty red bow on the top of the box. She pulled the card out and shined the flashlight on it, noting her name on the front in a masculine scrawl she recognized as Owen's handwriting. He must have sneaked the present in earlier.

Heart pounding, she opened the envelope and pulled out

the Christmas card with a hand-drawn picture on the front depicting Christ's birth in a manger as a brilliant star shone down from above.

With shaking hands, she opened the card.

Your mom would be proud of the mother you've become. Thank you for taking such good care of Janey. I'm sure she will never forget you.
Owen.

As her eyes burned, Sara set the card down and tore the red-and-green plaid paper off the gift, then opened the brown box inside and carefully pulled out several globs of crumpled tissue paper. She gasped. There, nestled down in more tissue paper and bubble wrap, lay the horse snowglobe like her mom's which Sara had pointed out to Owen the day they'd gone to The Snowglobe Gift Shoppe.

As tears fell to her cheeks, she gingerly turned the globe upside down and then righted it. Carefully she reached underneath and twisted the small metal winder a few times to make the music play.

Strains of "The Impossible Dream" lilted out as the horse danced, its mane seeming to fly in and out among the snowflakes as its hooves carried it through the drifts of snow. The words to the song wound their way through her head, resonating within her—to fight, to love, to try, to reach—and suddenly she came to a stunning realization. She hadn't done any of those things when Owen had left today. *None. Of. Them.*

Oh, sure, she'd made a feeble effort to change his mind. But basically she'd rolled over and accepted his decision, for his and the girls' sakes she'd told herself. And she hadn't had the courage or strength to tell him she'd go *wherever* to be with him.

But she saw now that she'd really capitulated and let him

walk out because it was the safe route, the one that wouldn't threaten her or force her to look her fears in the eye and kick them to the curb in the interest of her, and Owen's, lifelong happiness. Because she'd been hurt so very badly before.

She herself hadn't trusted in God's plan, either. Not enough to tell Owen she'd find a way to go to Moonlight Cove at the very least.

And suddenly she understood that happiness was there, right in front of her, for the taking. If she had the courage to dream the impossible dream.

She took a deep, shaky breath and set the snowglobe on the coffee table in front of her, watching as the snow settled. The horse was still running as the music died out, it's mane flying, it's delicate chin set at a stubborn angle as it looked forward, ready to go the distance, no matter what.

She raised her own chin. She needed to keep running, keep going after what would make her happy. She could not hide from the truth any longer.

She loved Owen, desperately so, and she was willing to own the emotion fully. And that meant she had to fight for their love with all she had, needed to tell him how she'd felt and that she would follow him anywhere. She'd go down swinging.

A quick glance at her watch told her it was just past seven. He hadn't told her when his flight left this evening. Could she catch him before he left town? She went for her cell phone and with trembling fingers brought up his number and pressed Dial, hoping against hope that she wouldn't be too late.

Just then, the power whirred back to life. Sara paused, looking around. The Christmas tree glowed anew with twinkling lights and the matching Tiffany lamps on the tables at each end of the couch lit the room with soft, multicolored hues.

Just as Owen had lit up her life.

And as her trust in God had illuminated her path.

She smiled, at peace with her decision. Yes. Having faith in the Lord's plan would be a blessing worth any risk.

Owen white-knuckled his truck's steering wheel as the falling snow swirled against the windshield and beyond, making visibility on the way to the Kalispell airport tricky. He'd switched into four-wheel drive a block from his house, but the truck still fishtailed periodically on the snow and ice building up on the roadway.

He'd sold the truck to Jeff and planned on buying a new one in Moonlight Cove. Jeff hadn't been able to take him to the airport tonight, so they'd agreed that Owen would leave the truck at the airport and Jeff would get it tomorrow when he picked up his in-laws who were flying in for the holidays.

Owen had hurriedly packed suitcases, leaving the rest for a moving company he'd hired. He then called the airline before he and Janey had left home just fifteen minutes ago, and his flight was still scheduled to depart on time. He was determined to be on the plane and away from Snowglobe by morning. A new life awaited him and Janey in Moonlight Cove, one without buckets of snow and frigid temperatures all winter long.

And without Sara.

He set his jaw, fighting the urge to turn the truck around. Once again, she'd impressed him to no end today. She'd kept it together when he and Janey had left Sara's house earlier, though he'd been able to tell from the tightness of her lips that she was struggling with his decision.

He was, too. It had been the hardest thing he'd ever done, walking away from her when he knew she wanted him to stay. But he had a path laid out, one that would keep his heart unscathed and his world in control.

He wished he could have seen her face when she opened the horse snowglobe. Had her eyes lit up with happiness as a brilliant smile graced her face? He'd meant every word he'd written in the note he'd left; he and Janey would never forget Sara.

With a renewed grip on the steering wheel he corrected the path of the truck slightly as it slipped sideways a bit. As he straightened the wheels and maintained good lane position away from the deep ditch on the side of the road, he told himself for the hundredth time that stepping off that path into the unknown was beyond him.

Wasn't it?

He looked off into the snow swirled darkness spreading out before him, noting the Christmas lights on the houses in the distance. People were tucked in tight in those houses, enjoying the holiday with loved ones. And he was…alone in this bleak, freezing night, on his way to a life in a place where he knew no one.

For a split second he cast his gaze to the backseat where Janey slept in her car seat. He loved his daughter with everything in him. Would protect her with his life, and would treasure every moment with her, no matter where they put down roots. But would that be enough, forever?

Would it?

That question reverberated in his brain, peppering him with nagging doubts, and he let out a heavy breath just as his cell phone rang from the front passenger seat. He glanced quickly but couldn't see the caller ID and decided to stay as safe as possible and not answer. If it was important, the caller would leave a message.

He shifted his gaze back to the road and immediately saw a panel truck in the oncoming lane sliding straight at them on the ice-slicked street. His gut bunched, spiking adrenaline into his system, and he instinctively jerked the wheel to the right. He overcorrected and braked too hard, and as the ice on the road took over, his rig lost traction, despite the anti-lock brakes clicking under his foot, and started a sideways slide of its own, out of the oncoming path of the other vehicle by a seeming hairsbreadth.

His heart thundering, Owen urged the steering wheel left to get his truck back on course and eased back on the brake a bit, but the action was useless against the slippery ice and snow on the road.

The truck slid and slid and slid, making a full three-sixty. Janey cried out, "Daddy!" and Owen could do nothing but hang on with a death grip, his eyes wide and his breath frozen in his lungs as the snow-covered scenery drifted by in seeming slow motion like a road-trip movie gone bad.

No control. No power. Nothing...

As his two-ton truck hurtled toward the ice-crusted ditch, spinning like a child's top across the frozen ground, he let up on the brake completely to unlock the wheels, and a silent prayer rose in his mind.

God, I give myself up to You...take control!

Another terror-filled second clicked by, and the wide ditch loomed wide in front of the truck's nose. With a *clunk* and a *whoosh* the vehicle went over the edge, careened down into the depression, and then came to a bone-crunching stop as the front fender rammed into the far side of the ditch.

With a devastatingly quick blast, the air bag deployed, and he felt as if he'd been hit by a brick wall. A nasty smell filled his throbbing nose, making him gag, and when he opened his eyes, what looked like white fog and dust surrounded him.

Was the truck on fire?

"Janey!" he shouted, twisting around as best he could. More dust filled the air, but he could see that Janey appeared unharmed, even though her eyes were round with fright.

"Daddy!" she cried, holding her arms out.

He tried to reach for her, but his seat belt restrained him, and besides, the airbag was in the way.

Panicked, he unhooked his seat belt and fumbled for the door handle. "I'm coming, sweetie. One second…" Wait, the truck was still in Drive…with shaking hands he tried to put it in Park, but it was stuck. Oh, yeah, the brake.

Finally, he found the brake and shifted into Park, realizing as he did so that the white dust was from the air bags. No fire…good.

He had to get to Janey. He swiped at the door handle, holding his breath against the smell, and managed to get the door cracked open.

Panting, he pushed at the door, but the truck had ended up on the upper side of the ditch on a sharp angle, so the door didn't want to stay open. With a burst of adrenaline that made his face pound, he muscled it open and crawled out as smoke-like fumes followed him into the freezing night air.

Snow pelted his face, stinging as it landed on his throbbing cheek, but he ignored the pain and focused on getting to Janey. He grabbed the crew cab door handle and yanked, praying it would open.

Thankfully, it gave way. Straining with its weight, he muscled some more and wedged his body between the door and the frame of the truck.

"Janey, are you all right?" he said, trying to stay calm. Pushing farther in, he hefted himself up and knelt on the truck seat, keeping the door open with his booted feet, then reached out and grabbed her mitten-clad hands.

She looked at him, pale-faced. "What happened, Daddy?"

He fumbled for the hook on her car seat; though it was bitterly cold outside, the smell from the airbag was too noxious to stay put. "We slid into the ditch."

"I scared, Daddy," she said in a trembling voice.

"Me, too, sweet pea, but everything is okay." He got the latch undone and lifted the Y restraint over her head. "I'm going to get you out of here and call a tow truck, okay?"

She patted his arm. "Okay. You call Sara, too?"

He paused, his jaw slack, then hefted her up slightly. "Um…you think I should call Sara?"

"'Course. She always makes us better. Right?"

The conviction and truth in his daughter's words landed on him with the force of an anvil. Sara did always make things better. Perfect, actually. "Right," he managed to shove out.

Determined to focus on the situation at hand, he scooched back. "Can you climb out of your seat and come over here so I can lift you out of the truck?"

"Uh-huh." She pushed herself up and out—

A knock on the crew cab window almost stopped his heart. He whipped around and saw an older man wearing a base-ball hat peering into the window, his face illuminated by the flashlight he held. The panel truck driver? Or another random motorist?

"You guys okay?" he hollered.

"Fine," Owen replied. "I need to get her out of here and then call a tow."

The man shined the flashlight into Owen's face. "Is that you, Owen?"

Owen blinked.

"It's me, Josiah Elfridge. You repaired my garage roof last winter."

Relief washed over Owen when he recognized Josiah. "Yeah, it's me, and my daughter, Janey."

"Thought I recognized you." Josiah peered closer. "Your face looks like it took a beating. I think I should call 911."

Owen reached up and pressed a hand to his throbbing nose. Zowie, that hurt. Could be broken. Hopefully just bruised. But his brain was fuzzy from the walloping the air bag had delivered, and it would be stupid not to be cautious when he had Janey to take care of. "Yeah, okay. But first, if you'll hold the door open a bit wider, I'll get her out."

Josiah obliged, and soon Owen was standing on the side of the road with Janey in his arms. His nose thudded in time with his heartbeat, and he felt a bit dizzy. The wind whipped snow around, pelting them, and Janey buried her head in his neck.

Josiah gestured to the panel truck slanted at an angle on the shoulder of the road about a hundred feet away. "Why don't you two come and sit in my truck while I call 911," he said, raising his voice to be heard over the wind. "I'd take you to the hospital myself, but these roads are treacherous right now, and I'm afraid we might not make it. We were both slip-sliding around here."

"I agree," Owen replied. "I was on my way to the airport."

Josiah motioned him in the direction from which Owen had come. "Guess you won't be making that flight, will you?"

"Guess not," Owen replied.

"You want me to take her?" Josiah asked, nodding toward Janey. "It's slick out here, and you took a pretty big hit to the noggin."

Owen shook his head, which started drumbeats pounding in his face. "No, I've got her." He put his mouth to Janey's ear underneath her hat. "This nice man, Josiah, is going to call for help."

"All right, Daddy. Then you call Sara."

Sara. Her pretty face rose in his mind, and he couldn't help but think about what a wonderful woman she was and how he couldn't imagine not having her in his life.

His chest tightened, and in that single moment in time, he realized he loved Sara.

Just as quickly, thoughts of those few moments when the truck had been sliding out of control flitted through his memory. He'd had no control, no power, and he'd given over to God automatically, trusting that He would save them, fulfilling His plan for Owen.

Maybe Owen needed to give his future up to God's plan, needed to trust in His power and wisdom, just as he'd had faith that the Lord would watch over him and Janey just a few minutes ago.

And that meant he had to tell Sara he loved her. And that she'd been right; he *had* been running away by leaving town.

But the truth was, he couldn't escape his love for Sara. No matter where he was, he'd love her. And she was his fresh start, his new life.

She was his everything.

As soon as he got checked out by a doctor, he planned to tell her all of it. He only hoped he hadn't scared her off with his running away routine. Or that she didn't love him back. Either way, at least he'd know that he didn't give up without a fight worthy of his newly recognized trust in God's plan, and of the woman who'd stolen his heart.

With Mia's hand clamped tightly in her own, Sara forced herself to slow down so Mia could keep up as they charged through the automatic sliding doors to the emergency room of the local hospital.

Concern thrumming inside her, Sara went immediately to the reception desk opposite the door. "I'm here to see Owen Larsen," she told the tall, thin nurse behind the desk. "He was admitted a few hours ago."

Owen had called half an hour ago, and she'd breathed a sigh of relief to hear his voice, because he hadn't been answering his cell and she was beyond worried about him and Janey. She'd also feared they were already on the plane to Seattle and were well and truly gone, and her heart had just about shattered.

Then he'd told her that they'd been in a car accident and were still in Snowglobe, albeit at the hospital, hurriedly assuring her that they were both fine except for his face being a little banged up by the air bag.

Sara's stomach had fallen to her toes the second she'd heard the word *accident,* confirming she should have never let him run away without more of a fight.

She had to believe in dreaming the impossible dream. How could she ask less of herself when so much was at stake?

Even though he'd wanted her to stay home because of the

icy roads, she'd adamantly refused. She'd grown up dealing with the inclement weather in Snowglobe, and life went on, snow or not. Besides, it wasn't far, and the roads had been salted.

Now, here she and Mia were at the hospital, safe and sound. Everything was fine, Sara knew, but she'd feel a lot better when she saw Owen and Janey with her own eyes.

The nurse consulted a chart. "Ah, yes. Mr. Larsen is just about to be discharged." She motioned to the waiting area. "If you want to have a seat, he'll be out shortly."

"Can I see him?" Sara asked in an anxiety-tinged voice.

"Are you family?"

"Well, no." And she never would be. Unless she could convince Owen to give them a chance. Mission noted. Again.

"Then I'm sorry, hospital policy prohibits you from going into the E.R. area." The nurse lifted a brow, then looked back down at the chart. "But I assure you, Mr. Larsen is just fine."

"And what about his daughter?" Sara knew Janey was fine physically, but she had to be scared out of her mind given what had gone on in the past few hours.

"One of the nurses was just out and told me that Janey is with her dad, and is the proud new owner of a new stuffed bear, so she's doing well," the nurse replied with a gentle smile. "I promise."

Nodding, Sara breathed a sigh of relief. When in doubt, give a kid a stuffed animal. "Okay, good." Knowing she'd have to cool her jets and settle for waiting for Owen, she turned to head over to the waiting area. "Let's go sit down, Mia."

"Where's Janey?" Mia asked, her voice small.

Before Sara could answer, the double doors leading to the E.R. swung open and Owen walked out.

Sara's heart stopped when she saw his bruised, puffy face. He looked like he'd tangled with a prizefighter rather than a vehicle safety device.

A plump older nurse followed behind with Janey in her arms.

Sara stared, drinking in the sight of him, all of her love for him bubbling up like a geyser inside of her.

His gaze caught hers, and his pained expression softened as his mouth curved into an unmistakable smile. Like frosting on a hot cinnamon roll, Sara's heart just about melted.

A second later, Janey spotted her, too, and cried out, "Sara!"

Sara moved toward the man and girl she loved, her eyes burning. And was utterly relieved when Owen stepped toward her and instantly, unhesitatingly, pulled her into his embrace. "I'm so glad you made it," he said. "After what happened to us, I was worried."

She put her arms around him and hugged him tight, motioning for the nurse to bring Janey over to join in, not caring a whit that he smelled like what had to be air-bag debris. "I know my way around in the snow," she said, never wanting to let either of them go. This was where she belonged, with him, wherever, and she had to tell him that. They'd been given a second chance, and she wasn't about to squander it. Oh, no. Never again.

However, now wasn't the time nor the place for the I-love-you-and-I'm-never-letting-you-out-of-my-sight discussion she intended to have. But she promised herself that the time and place would come about very soon.

And if Owen thought he could run away again, he had another think coming.

By the time Sara's car headlights illuminated the snow-covered For Rent sign in Owen's front yard, his nose had stopped throbbing, thanks, he was sure, to the large dose of ibuprofen the E.R. doc had given him.

Thankfully, an examination had revealed that his nose was not broken, just badly bruised, along with his whole face. He'd had his bell rung good for sure, but it could have been so much worse; just thinking about what might have been made his knees weak.

Thank You, God, for watching over Janey and me. And for helping me to see what's important. And what doesn't matter in the least.

The hospital had loaned them a car seat for Janey, since he hadn't had the foresight in his dazed state to grab his from the truck, which had been towed to a local body shop thanks to Josiah making a call. Owen would contact them tomorrow about repairs.

The girls were sound asleep in the backseat of Sara's car—it was near midnight, and both were understandably exhausted—and as he looked over at Sara and saw the soft curve of her face, cloaked in nighttime shadows, he knew he had to level with her. Now. And no matter what she said, he would rest easy knowing he'd trusted the Lord's plan enough to battle hard for the woman he loved.

How could that be a mistake?

The car came to a stop, and Sara shoved the gearshift into Park. She sat for a moment, her hands still on the wheel, and then turned and looked at him, her face pressed into serious lines. "We need to talk."

He lifted his eyebrows. Looked like she had something on her mind, too. Okay. He'd face it head-on, no more running away. His neck heated up and he unzipped his coat. "I agree."

She blinked, paused, and then said, "First off, thank you for the snowglobe. It's the best present anyone has ever given me."

"You're welcome. I knew having it would mean a lot to you."

"It did." She fanned her face, then reached up and turned the heater control knob down.

"Warm?"

"Um…yeah."

"Me, too." There was so much to be said, so many hurdles

to clear...no, not anymore. The hard part was behind him. From here on out he'd have the comfort of his faith in God's guidance. *I'm free.*

With that wonderful thought in mind, feeling as if a huge load had been lifted from his shoulders, Owen reached out and pried Sara's hand off the steering wheel. "Sara, look at me."

She turned, gazed at him with a crease between her eyebrows, and opened her mouth to speak.

He pressed a finger to her lips. "No, don't say anything before I tell you something very important."

She gave him a slow, slightly shaky nod.

With a steady hand, he touched her cheek. "I love you, Sara Kincaid, and I never should have left."

Her jaw dropped and her eyes went the size of dinner plates as she gripped his hand, hard. "You do?" she whispered.

"I do." Hopefully, someday not too far in the future, he'd be saying those words in a church, with Sara outfitted in a gorgeous white dress standing by his side, with God looking on, happy that Owen had recognized the perfection of His plan. But first things first.

"I thought—"

"That I was going to run away?"

"Yes." She nodded. "That's right."

"I was."

Her eyebrows crinkled. "Then...what changed your mind?" she asked in an awestruck voice.

"God did." At her seemingly stunned silence, he continued on. "When my truck was spinning out of control on the ice, my worst fear came true. And in that space of time, I gave myself up to God's control and that made me realize that I needed to trust in His plan for my life." He brought her hand to his mouth and kissed her knuckles. "I think you're God's plan for me and that He brought us together, and I can't ignore that anymore."

She let out a gasp, and then her hand tightened on his again and she turned in her seat to face him fully. Her expression was soft with a small smile curving her lips. "Can you guess what I wanted to tell you?"

"I know what I *want* you to tell—"

She mimicked him and pressed a finger to his lips to silence him. "I love you, too, and I knew when I opened that snowglobe and listened to 'The Impossible Dream' that I had to follow *my* dream, no matter how impossible it seemed." She sucked in a trembling breath. "When you called to tell me you'd been in an accident and my heart just about froze with fear...well, it was clear, then and there, that my decision to fight for you was the right one." She cast her eyes into the backseat where Janey and Mia slept, oblivious to the momentous event playing out just feet from them. "For all of us. And that means I'll find a way to go to Moonlight Cove if that's what will keep us together."

Pure joy exploded in his heart. He twisted and leaned down toward Sara, resting his forehead on hers, careful to keep his nose safe as he did so. "You'd do that?"

"For you?" She nuzzled his jaw. "Anything."

The depth of her sacrifice humbled him. What had he done to deserve such a wonderful woman? "No, now that I've found you, I realize I want to stay in Snowglobe."

"Even with your sad memories?" she asked, her voice hushed.

"I have new, happy memories here, and I want to make more," he said. "With you and Mia, as a family."

"Are you sure?"

"I've never been more sure of anything in my life."

"Neither have I," Sara said on a breathy sigh.

He gave her a teasing grin. "So are you telling me we're on the same page, Miss Kincaid?"

She smiled back, stroking a soft hand down his cheek. "I believe we are, Mr. Larsen."

"That's the best news I've had in quite a while," he said. "In forever, actually."

Then he kissed her sweet lips for a long time, never wanting to let her go.

And now, thanks to God, some black ice and the most wonderful woman in the world, Owen wouldn't have to.

Thank you, dear Lord, for making all of our Christmas wishes come true.

* * * * *

Dear Reader,

I love writing about small towns, so when I was asked to write a novella that took place in a little Montana town call Snowglobe, I jumped at the chance. Somehow I find romance so much more heartfelt and genuine when set against the backdrop of a close-knit community.

An interesting thing happened recently—a friend read one of my books and told me that she could tell that I had based some of the happenings in that book on my real-life experiences. She also shared that she thought the tangible connection between the events in my books and my life experience had added another layer to the genuineness of the story.

I thought about that, and right about the time I wrote the scene where Owen, Sara, Mia and Janey are arriving at The Snowglobe Gift Shoppe and Sara asks the girls to hold their hands behind their backs to remind themselves not to touch anything, I realized my friend was right. Here's why: my mom always asked my kids to clasp their hands behind their backs whenever there were fragile things in sight. That realization made me feel good. You see, my mom died in 2006, and I miss her every day. But somehow I'm comforted to know that my mom, in her own way, has contributed to the authenticity and multidimensional quality of the events in my books.

Thanks, Mom.

Hearing from readers is always a joy. So please, let me know how you like my books. You can contact me via Harlequin Love Inspired Books, or on the web at lissa@lissamanley.com.

Blessings,
Lissa Manley

Questions for Discussion

1. Owen wanted control of his life after his wife died. Was this choice limiting in a negative way, or was it an inevitable result of the tragic event he'd been through? Discuss why or why not, and how you might have reacted in a similar situation, and whether you feel, given time, Owen might have learned to give up some control of his life even if he hadn't met Sara.

2. Because Sara's dad and husband walked out on her, she didn't want to depend on anyone for fear of being hurt. Was this a wrongheaded way to go about things, and if so, how could she have reacted differently? Or was her reaction understandable, and, therefore, justified, even though it limited her ability to let someone into her heart, and, ultimately, her own possible chances for happiness?

3. Sara told Owen she didn't think he was trusting in God's plan, and that he was letting his need for control in actuality control him. Discuss the veracity of this idea, and whether you think this was what Owen was doing, and whether this reaction was justified given the loss that he suffered.

4. Sara hoped that Owen would stay in Snowglobe to be with her, yet she wasn't initially willing to move to Moonlight Cove to stay together. Listening to the musical horse snowglobe play "The Impossible Dream" helped her to realize the error in her thinking. Discuss how a song or other artistic work has influenced you in a positive way.

5. In church, Owen was nervous to let Janey go to Sunday school class, even though he undoubtedly knew that doing so was in his daughter's best interest. Discuss how you have had to let go in this way, and whether or not it was the right thing to do in the long run.

6. Owen and Sara discussed having faith in the Lord's plan. Discuss times in your life when you trusted in the Lord's plan even though doing so didn't come easily for you, and how that trust helped you deal in subsequent times of crisis.

7. It took some black ice and a spinout into a ditch to show Owen that he actually trusted in the Lord. Discuss how a similarly traumatic or frightening experience shaped your view of your faith and trust in God.

REQUEST YOUR FREE BOOKS!

2 FREE INSPIRATIONAL NOVELS
PLUS 2
FREE
MYSTERY GIFTS

LIREG11B

celebrating 15 YEARS

Love Inspired

USA TODAY bestselling author

JILLIAN HART

brings you the final installment of

— TEXAS TWINS —

Twenty-five years ago Dr. Brian Wallace and Belle Colby were married with two sets of twins—toddler boys and infant girls. Then the young family was torn apart. Each took a girl and boy and went their separate ways—never to see one another again. Brian is stunned to return home from a mission to find all the siblings reunited at their mother's Texas ranch. Will unanswered questions stand in the way of this family finding their long-awaited second chance?

Reunited for the Holidays

Available November 13 from Love Inspired Books!

celebrating
15 YEARS

Love Inspired™

Discover a second chance at love with author

Lois Richer

Helping children in her hometown is a dream fulfilled
for single mother Brianna Benson. But being back
in Hope, New Mexico, isn't easy for the medical
clinic's new child psychologist. Ten years ago, Brianna
discovered that her fiancé, Zac Enders, betrayed her—
and she left town in tears. Now a school administrator,
Zac is asking for her help with kids at risk. But how
can she work with the man who broke her heart?
As Christmas approaches, the gift of reunited love is
waiting to be unwrapped.

Yuletide Proposal

Available November 13 from Love Inspired Books.

www.LoveInspiredBooks.com

LI87783